Fountain
of Life

Rebecca Martin

Christian Light Publications, Inc.
Harrisonburg, Virginia 22802

FOUNTAIN OF LIFE

Christian Light Publications, Inc.
Harrisonburg, Virginia 22802
© 2001 by Christian Light Publications, Inc.
All rights reserved. Published 2001
Printed in the United States of America

Fourth Printing, 2011

Cover by David W. Miller

ISBN: 978-0-87813-595-0

*"Whosoever drinketh of the water
that I shall give him shall never
thirst; but the water that
I shall give him shall be in him
a well of water springing up into
everlasting life."* –Jesus

John 4:14

Table of Contents

Jewish Calendar

	Months		Feasts	Farming
Numerical	Babylonian	Modern Equivalent	Feasts	Farming
First	Nisan (Abib)*	Mar-April	Passover Feast of Unleavened Bread	Begin barley harvest, latter rains
Second	Iyyar (Ziv)*	Apr-May		Barley harvest
Third	Sivan	May-June	Feast of Weeks/Pentecost	Wheat harvest, vine tending
Fourth	Tammuz	June-July		
Fifth	Ab	July-Aug		Grapes, figs, olives ripen
Sixth	Elul	Aug-Sept		Grape harvest begins
Seventh	Tishri (Ethanim)*	Sept-Oct	Feast of Trumpets/New Year Day of Atonement Feast of Tabernacles	Early rains, plowing, olive harvest
Eighth	Marchesvan (Bul)*	Oct-Nov		Barley planting
Ninth	Kislev	Nov-Dec	Feast of Lights/ Dedication of Temple	Grain planting
Tenth	Tebeth	Dec-Jan		Rainy winter months
Eleventh	Shebat	Jan-Feb		Almond trees bloom
Twelfth	Adar	Feb-Mar	Festival of Purim	Citrus fruit harvest

*Canaanite names in parentheses.

Jerusalem in the Time of Jesus

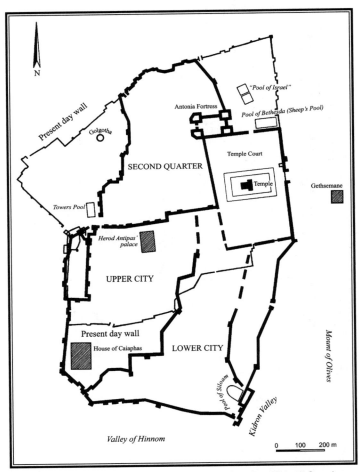

Yuval and Shlomit Greenbaum

Herod's Temple

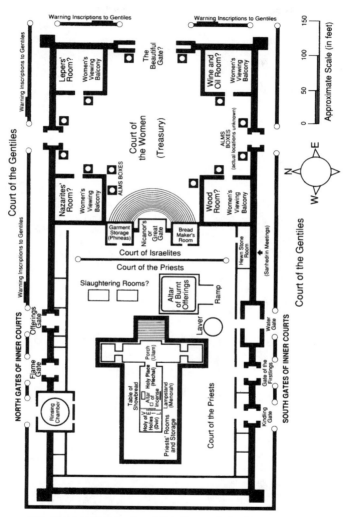

From Son Light Bible Map Insert. Used by permission. For more information go to www.sonlightpublishers.com.

Fountain of Life, set in New Testament times, vividly portrays the controversy and strong feelings among people searching to determine who Jesus really was.

In keeping with Christian Light Publications' Bible times policy, the characters and incidents in this account are in harmony with Scripture, but there is no interaction with Bible characters. There should be no confusion between this story and the Bible record.

Parents and teachers will appreciate the book's educational value. It presents life in Jesus' time, as well as lessons in Old Testament Law, feasts, and holy days. It also includes a Jewish calendar and a glossary of terms.

For many today the controversy over Jesus' identity continues. We trust *Fountain of Life* will inspire you and your friends to read the Bible also, through which you can deepen your personal acquaintance with Jesus. He is, indeed, the Fountain of Life, who quenches the thirst of all who come to Him and drink.

–The Publishers

Chapter 1

Dark rain clouds were gathering in the sky above the Judean hills. The month was Adar, the last of the Jewish sacred year, and the time of the latter rains. As the first drops began to fall, two young men were hurrying down the Mount of Olives toward Jerusalem, drawing their billowing cloaks more tightly about them.

Eli, the younger of the two, turned to his companion with a wry smile and began chanting a passage from the Torah. "'But the land, whither ye go to possess it, is a land of hills and valleys, and drinketh water of the rain of heaven.'"

Hesitantly at first, then more confidently as the passage came back to him, Jacob joined in: "'A land which the Lord thy God careth for: the eyes of the Lord thy God are always upon it, from the beginning of the year even unto the end of the year. And it shall come to pass, if ye shall hearken diligently unto my commandments which I command you this day, to love the Lord your God, and to serve him with all your heart and with all your soul, That I will give you the rain of your land in his due season, the first rain and the latter rain, that thou mayest gather in thy corn, and thy wine, and thine oil.'"

Jacob drew a corner of his cloak over his thick, dark hair as the rain became heavier. "For one who hates studying as much as you seem to, you quote Scripture well."

"I remember that passage because it's about things I really care for," Eli explained. "It's about the land, and farming, and harvest." He sighed. "But studying the Law, with all those 613 statutes, and the endless commentary—what a heavy burden that is when I would rather be out in Joel's vineyard!"

Jacob shook his head. "I will never understand you. Your father makes great sacrifices so that you can go to the rabbinical school. After a few more years of study, you could be a learned and honored rabbi. Yet you'd rather work in the rain on a muddy hillside, building terraces so that a rich Sadducee can grow richer by producing more grapes!"

Eli shrugged sadly. "And you, who don't have to go to rabbinical school, but may work on the land every day, consider me a privileged man. What an upside-down world!"

"I feel sorry for your father," Jacob said seriously. "His whole heart is set on seeing you succeed where he failed because of his illness. He doesn't want you to be an unskilled laborer. He looks at you, his only child, and dreams of seeing you a second Hillel, a prince of the Sanhedrin, a teacher of thousands!"

"I can never fulfill his dreams!" Eli said in anguish. "I'm no longer a child. I'm nineteen years old. When will Father realize? When will he understand that I grow weary of endless lessons, the endless studying of the Law and the prophets? My hands were meant to hold a shovel or a scythe, not fragile parchment scrolls in gloomy schoolrooms." He held up one hand, dirty from the afternoon of terrace-building.

Jacob shook his head. "If only I had the chance you have! I would grasp the opportunity to live a life of ease among books, away from backbreaking toil in other men's vineyards and olive groves."

Eli turned his face away as tears mingled with the rain on his face.

Sensitive to his friend's feelings, Jacob's voice softened. "Look, Eli, Zion! I never reach this spot where Jerusalem comes into view without being filled with awe."

Eli drew a hand across his cheeks and turned his gaze to the panorama below. Even though no setting sun transformed Jerusalem into a "city of gold" this evening, the vast spread of limestone buildings was an impressive sight. High on Mount Zion, with its array of marble and gold, the magnificent temple gleamed even without the sunlight.

"I see this every day," Jacob mused, "yet it never fails to take my breath away. How must it be for the Passover pilgrims who come only once a year, or even once in a lifetime?"

Eli nodded. "Today, the city seems asleep, but soon she will awaken as the thousands of pilgrims come here next month for Passover." They descended into the dark shadows of the valley just beneath the city wall to cross the Kidron brook.

"Better hurry," said Jacob. "The gates will soon be closing."

They shouldered their way among a knot of people crowding through the massive gate and hurried along the winding streets to the poor section, called the Lower City. Here the streets were so narrow that Eli could easily touch the walls on both sides at once. Lights were winking on in the windows of the flat-roofed limestone houses crowded one against the other.

A shout rang through the shadowy street. A small figure hurtled out of a doorway, shouting, "Jacob! You're home at last! Why are you so late?" In a flurry of arms and legs, the boy flung himself upon his older brother.

Eli watched with a twinge of envy as the two disappeared, hand in hand, into the House Ben Josiah. Though his parents would be glad to see him, there would not be an enthusiastic welcome. He strode on, quickly covering the short distance to his own home, the House Ben Amos.

About to duck through the low doorway, he pulled back, startled. From the courtyard came a man's voice.

"Well, Amos," the voice said, "I hope this has not been too upsetting for you. The other rabbis and I agreed it was time you knew of the situation. Let us know if there is something we can do. Shalom."

Eli sucked in his breath sharply. He knew that voice! It was the Rabbi Jedekiah, his teacher! What could he want here, at his father's house, this time of day?

The rabbi almost brushed against the young man shrinking against the wall without noticing him. "Oh, shalom," he said apologetically. This Jewish greeting, meaning "Peace be to you," passed for both hello and good-bye. "You are back from your work on the terraces, I see."

4

"Yes," said Eli respectfully, not knowing what else to say.

The rabbi nodded curtly and swept on down the street.

Eli's knees trembled as he entered the courtyard. Everything seemed as usual. Mother stood near the brazier just inside the house, stirring a pot of lentil soup while the smoke curled out the doorway. She turned quickly upon hearing Eli's step in the stone courtyard.

"You are late, Eli," she said.

"We were busy till the last minute, finishing a terrace," Eli explained. He held his hands over the brazier, soaking up the warmth and breathing in the aroma of cooking lentils.

"And enjoying every minute of it, I'm sure," she said with a hint of reproach.

Eli knew why. His parents had not really wanted him to take the afternoon job with Joel. They would rather have had him studying at home each day, thus hastening the time when he would be a teacher. But, because Eli had begged—and because they were hard-pressed for money—they had given in.

"Yes, Mother, you are right. I enjoyed it," he admitted humbly.

She shook her head. "Working in the cold and wet and dirt, when you could be indoors learning more about the great Law of God!"

Her words troubled him more than Jacob's had. *What is the matter with you?* she seemed to be asking. It was a question Eli often asked himself. Why didn't he share his father's great reverence for the

Law? Why was he not more interested in the God whom his father worshiped? What would Father think if he knew that Eli sometimes wondered whether God existed?

"Go in and wash," Mother said kindly. "Your father is waiting to see you."

Eli passed to the inner room. By the light of the olive-oil lamp he could make out the figure of his father, sitting cross-legged on the floor. Across his lap sprawled the canvas of a tent he had been mending. But Father's fingers, warped by a crippling disease, lay motionless on the canvas, and his head hung so that his chin rested on his chest.

When he heard Eli, he slowly raised his head. The pain in the sunken eyes struck Eli like a blow. He knew instantly it was not merely physical pain—though Father often suffered severely. There was another pain, something brought on, no doubt, by Rabbi Jedekiah's visit. "You are home," Father said dully.

"Yes, Father." Eli folded his strong legs and sat near him, longing to somehow soothe the pain. He wondered what his teacher's visit had been about. He knew it could be a while before his parents talked about it— if they ever would.

Mother came in, bearing the pot of steaming soup. Father gestured impatiently. "My prayer shawl," he demanded sharply.

Eli hastened to bring him the tasseled garment so precious to the Pharisees. He drew his own shawl about him, and they began chanting the prayers for the evening meal. At last it was time to eat, and Eli dipped his bread eagerly into the dish, using it as a sop to bring the soup to his mouth. He was so hungry that for awhile he did not mind his parents' heavy silence.

By the end of the meal, they still had not spoken about Jedekiah's visit. When Eli could bear the oppressive silence no longer, he drew on his cloak and went up the wooden ladder to the housetop.

The rain had stopped, and myriads of stars dusted the sky above Jerusalem. The lights in the dwellings seemed to be reflecting them below.

Eli looked up, thinking, *Somewhere up there is where God is supposed to be. I wonder who He is? If I were to try harder to fulfill my father's dreams, and study day and night, would I be able to understand God? Is He really to be found among musty old scrolls? I feel nearer to Him here, or when I am in the groves and fields, than when I am at school.*

There was a rustling sound as Mother came up the ladder to join him. "Father's asleep. But he said I may tell you about . . . about the rabbi's visit."

"I was wondering about it," Eli said.

"It was just such a terrible blow," Mother explained. She huddled against the low wall, seeking shelter from the damp wind. "I suppose we should have seen it coming. We knew you took more interest in farming than in book learning. Still, we could not bring ourselves to believe that you would really give up the chance to become a rabbi."

"I won't, Mother," Eli said earnestly. "I am still willing to try. What is it? Is Jedekiah demanding more money for tuition?"

She shook her head. "No, it isn't that. It's that Jedekiah has given up on you. He says your interest is not in the right place. He says it is a waste of time for him to try to teach you more about the Law when so many others are eagerly awaiting the chance."

An incredible mixture of feelings rushed through Eli as he listened. There was sadness for his parents' disappointment. There was shame for his failure. Yet, at the same time there was an almost overwhelming sense of relief. For months, even years, he had struggled to fulfill his parents' expectations, yet deep down he had always feared he would fail, and that fear had been a tremendous burden. Now that the fear had become reality, it was, strangely, like a burden rolling from his young shoulders.

But the burden had fallen now upon his parents. "What shall we do?" wailed Mother. "We cannot keep on renting this house. It is Jedekiah's, and he was letting us have it as a loan which you would repay once you became a rabbi. If you leave his school, we must leave this house. In fact . . ." Her voice had become a moan. "We may have to leave Jerusalem. Rent is so high in the city."

As she spoke, an idea came to Eli, leaving him breathless. "Just the other day, Mother, I heard of a man advertising for more hired help when the barley harvest begins next month. I could work for him. He lives in Ashbaroth. We could move out there!" The words tumbled from him eagerly.

"Ashbaroth!" Mother spat out the word. "A tiny village ten miles from the city?" She spoke as though going there would be the ultimate exile.

Eli's shoulders slumped. He should have known his parents wouldn't want to leave the great city of their birth. To him, the city, with its massive limestone walls, had often seemed a prison. "The landowner needing more help is called Simeon," he said.

Mother nodded. "Simeon the Sadducee. Do you, the son of a Pharisee, not shrink from working for a rich Sadducee?"

Eli shrugged. "Joel is one too. I guess I am not a very good Pharisee, because I can never make much sense out of the rivalry between the two sects."

Mother stared. "Surely you know the Sadducees' blasphemous beliefs, or lack of beliefs they would be better called! They refuse to accept anything but the five books of Moses and have no reverence for our prophets. They have no use for all our splendid laws . . ."

"That's right." Eli nodded. "The Sadducees consider them little more than man-made traditions, I guess." He dared not tell her he sometimes wondered if the Sadducees were right, and the Pharisees were carrying a vast, unnecessary burden with their 613 added statutes and laws.

Chapter 2

The notes of the *shofar* floated down the narrow street as Eli Bar Amos went home from work some weeks later in the month of Nisan. The young man smiled to himself. The ram's horn of Ashbaroth was a poor imitation of the ones used at the temple in Jerusalem. Its notes sounded flat and lame compared to the temple *shofars,* which sounded like liquid gold. Still, the message was the same: the Passover Sabbath was nearing!

Eli quickened his step. He looked forward to the evening's festivities, eating the paschal meal with a company of relatives and friends. After only two weeks in their new home, he was surprised at how many of the villagers he already knew. Some of them had been faintly familiar because they were cousins of his parents. Uncle Shem, Father's half brother, also lived in Ashbaroth with his family. The rest had been strangers, but now they were friends. They had all helped the family of Amos get settled in the home provided by the landowner Simeon.

The house would be crowded tonight. The Law said

at least ten men were needed to make a company for the paschal meal; and since each of those ten men brought wives and children, several dozen would be gathered! People were already entering the courtyard, wearing festive smiles and calling "shalom" to each other. From within came the aroma of roast lamb.

Once everyone was gathered and sitting on the floor around the crude table, the ceremonies began. Eli watched his father. There was a longing look on his face. He was remembering other Passovers in Jerusalem when they had been able to sacrifice their lamb properly at the temple. Eli ached for his parents. If only they could be as happy as he was in their new home, doing the work he loved, freed from the confines of schoolrooms!

Crippled though he was, Father could still perform the paschal rites. First he blessed the wine; and when everyone had drained his cup, they rose for a ceremonial hand-washing. Then the rest of the meal, with its bitter herbs and unleavened bread, was brought to the table.

Eli cleared his throat nervously. At this point the son of the house had a part. He was to ask the Five Questions asking the reasons for eating this special meal. Could he repeat them flawlessly? Father would be displeased if he did not.

Licking his dry lips, Eli began, "Why is this night different from all other nights...?"

Father answered instantly, fluently, reciting the history of Israel from Abraham on through the captivity in Egypt. But by the time Eli had asked the Third Question, Father's strength began to flag, and Uncle

Shem's dry, grating voice took over, telling the story of the First Passover.

Some of the younger children were getting tired of sitting and looking at the food. Mothers tried to stifle their children's whimpers. A baby let out a lusty wail.

Though nearly drowned out, Uncle Shem kept on unflinchingly. Eli suppressed a smile. He could sympathize with the children. He was hungry too! Finally it was time to eat, but carefully, following the prescribed customs, stopping at certain points to drink wine. After the fourth cup of wine, they sang a portion of the Hallel (Psalms 113—118), which signaled the end of the ceremony.

The men began visiting among themselves in undertones. Uncle Shem had leaned back against the wall, his eyes half closed. Eli noticed one voice above the rest. Craning his neck, he recognized the speaker as Aaron, who, like many of the villagers, also worked for Simeon.

"You mean you haven't heard?" he asked. "Well, it is hard to believe, but it must be true. I was told by someone who claimed he saw it for himself."

Aaron settled himself more comfortably, preparing to tell the story that suddenly had everyone's attention. "You all know the temple is a busy place just before the Passover, with all those pilgrims getting their money changed and buying animals for sacrifices. Things were busy as usual in the marketplace, when suddenly a man came in and started upsetting the moneychangers' tables! He had a whip, which He used to chase out oxen and sheep. Things happened so fast that people just stood there with their mouths hanging open."

"What did he think he was doing, anyway?" someone asked.

"The stranger said, 'Take these things away; do not make my Father's house a house of merchandise.' "

The room became silent at the strange words.

"Who was this man?" Father asked finally.

"They call him Jesus," Aaron replied.

"Hmmm," said another. "Was not a Man named Jesus linked with the one called John the Baptist?"

Aaron nodded. "The same. So you heard of Him."

"A little," replied the other. "There was a strange story about a voice from heaven when this Jesus was baptized by John."

Filled with wonder, Eli strained to hear.

"Did our rulers imprison this Jesus after such irreverent behavior at the temple?" Eli's father asked angrily.

Aaron shook his head. "I was told when they asked Jesus why He had done this thing, He gave another strange answer: 'Destroy this temple, and in three days I will raise it up.' "

"Sounds like a lunatic," someone growled.

Aaron shrugged. "I don't know. It took 46 years to build that temple. At any rate, I understand Nicodemus is going to check out this fellow."

"Nicodemus will get to the root of the matter," Father said with satisfaction. Eli knew Father held Nicodemus in high esteem.

Soon parting shaloms rang out as people began going home. Father courteously thanked the guests for coming. But Eli knew his father was thinking how much better it would be celebrating the Passover in the Holy City itself.

14

After the last guest had gone, Eli lingered in the courtyard, his mind replaying Aaron's story. He felt a strange mixture of excitement and foreboding. Who really was this Jesus?

When Mother came out, he asked her, "What were they talking about—that voice from heaven? Had you heard about that?"

In the moonlight he detected a frown on her face. "Yes, we had heard a little something about it, but Father forbade me to tell you. You knew about John the Baptist before tonight though, didn't you?"

"Yes, of course," Eli answered. "He calls people to repentance and baptizes them in the Jordan River. The Pharisees don't approve, but they can't stop people from flocking to him."

"Did you know John prophesies of a coming kingdom?" Mother asked softly. "Many people believe John is the one sent by God to herald the Messiah?"

Eli was electrified. "Really? And a voice from heaven came upon Jesus? Is He the One—the Messiah? But why wouldn't Father have wanted me to know?"

Mother sighed. "Don't get excited, Eli. Father is convinced there is nothing to the matter. So many different men have claimed to be the Messiah in recent years. Yet what was their end? You know as well as I do that the Romans crucify anyone who pretends to be king."

Eli nodded sadly. Israel, he knew, was a people in waiting, waiting for the King who would set the nation free from the Romans. "So Father thinks this Jesus is no better than the rest," he murmured, shuffling toward the house.

Mother's voice reached him through the darkness. "Father is probably right. This Jesus comes from Nazareth of Galilee. You know what the Scriptures say about the birthplace of the Messiah." Her tone turned brisk. "It's time you went to sleep, Eli. Tomorrow is the Feast of Firstfruits. Not that it will amount to much of a feast, here in this back-country place. Still, we will observe the day, even if we are far from the temple."

Eli groped for the ladder and clambered up to his tiny bedroom. Up until now, he had had no regrets about not being in Jerusalem for the Passover. But tonight, he found himself wishing he could be in the city tomorrow. Not because of the Feast—but because something within him longed for a glimpse of that man Jesus!

Chapter 3

The neighbors had offered to carry Father on his pallet to the synagogue, but he chose to stay home the next morning, pleading weariness from the Passover festivities. Eli suspected part of the reason was because a Passover service at a little village synagogue was hardly good enough for one accustomed to the splendid temple ceremonies. But Eli was quite happy to join the neighboring family as they walked to the synagogue at the top of the sloping street. Isaiah, the father, was a tall man in his forties. His wife was Leah. Their oldest son, Joseph, was near Eli's age. Next to him was a girl named Hannah, and then there was eight-year-old Isaac.

Already Isaac and Joseph were like brothers to Eli. His heart warmed as Isaac took his hand and remarked, "Today seems almost like a Sabbath. Nobody's doing any work."

"That's because the Law says the 15th of Nisan is to be held as a Sabbath," Eli informed him.

Isaac nodded. "But at the temple in Jerusalem, there will be even more sacrifices than on a Sabbath, won't there?"

"Two bullocks, a ram, seven lambs, and a goat," Eli recited from memory. "And hundreds of voluntary offerings besides."

"Voluntary offerings?" Isaac repeated questioningly.

"Ah, you know what they are," his brother put in impatiently. "Every male appearing before the Lord today must bring an offering. That's what all those pilgrims did that we watched on their way up to Jerusalem last week."

"Does everyone offer a lamb?" Isaac asked.

Isaiah shook his head. "Oh, no. Poor people like us would offer only a pigeon."

"We can't afford elaborate offerings like the rich people. Yet we are the ones who work hard, while they sit around growing fat on the fruit of our labors," Joseph said sarcastically.

"You sound like my friend Jacob Bar Josiah, back in Jerusalem," Eli told him laughingly.

After the service at the synagogue, Eli stood among the men outside. "There was a story," one of them said, "of a wedding feast in Cana of Galilee. Jesus was invited . . ."

From the crowd came a guffaw. "I heard that one too. You don't mean to say you believed it?"

The first speaker looked pained. "I'm not saying what I believe, only repeating what I heard. They ran out of wine before the festivities were over. After Jesus had servants fill several jars to the brim with water, He told them to draw some from the jars and carry it to the governor of the feast. When they did, the water had turned to wine!"

More laughter rose from the men. But Eli did not feel like laughing. He was ready to go home. He turned away, looking for Isaiah and the others. Once more his heart was strangely stirred by this story about Jesus.

PASSOVER WEEK was like a week of Sabbaths. The next morning Eli joined Isaiah's family to go to the synagogue.

"This is more fun than going to school," Isaac confided to Eli. "Did you know they will present the first barley sheaf to the Lord today?"

Eli smiled down at him. "Yes, I knew."

"But what does this Feast of the Firstfruits really mean?" Isaac wanted to know.

Eli looked at the boy's father. Isaiah began patiently, "Well, you know the barley and the wheat have been growing all winter while the rains fell. Now the barley is almost ready to be cut." He pointed to a field visible down in the valley below Ashbaroth. "See, it is white for harvest. But no sickle may be taken to the grain before the Lord has received His share—the firstfruits."

"And how are the firstfruits given to God?" Isaac persisted.

Joseph's eyes met Eli's over the little fellow's head, as if to say, "He is quite a question box."

Isaiah replied, "At sundown last night, three men went out and cut an ephah of barley. They threshed it, then parched and ground the grains until they had an omer of flour. Today this flour will be held up and waved before the Lord by the priests in the temple, and a handful of it will be offered on the altar."

Isaac nodded, satisfied.

When they reached the synagogue, Eli's eyes roved over the crowd. "Doesn't the landowner Simeon worship here? I have not seen him at the synagogue since we've lived in Ashbaroth."

"Oh, no, this village has another synagogue, down beyond that grove." Joseph pointed to citrus trees partway down the hill. "Haven't you seen their elegant building? It was built by the rich, for the rich. They would not want to mingle with us in our peasant robes," he said resentfully.

Eli nodded, then turned his attention to the talk around him. People were still discussing Jesus, what He had done at the temple, and other things He was rumored to have done.

"He can heal cripples with a touch," one man declared from beneath his tasseled prayer shawl.

"He can restore sight to the blind!" another maintained.

Each new revelation somehow thrilled Eli's soul. When he returned home, he went to his father. "They say Jesus can heal the sick! What if He were to come here and heal you?" he said impulsively.

Father had been lying listlessly on his pallet. Now he started up, his eyes wide. "Does my own son talk like that about this imposter? Don't you realize Jesus is nothing but a rebel who will bring more bloodshed upon us?"

Eli fell back as though he had received a blow. "I'm sorry, Father. I will not talk to you like that again."

Gloomily he climbed to the housetop. Here he could gaze out over the valley, shining with ripened grain. His heart lifted as he thought of the harvest about to begin. Soon he would be doing the work he had always longed to do!

His thoughts returned to Father, lying ill on his pallet. His sickness seemed worse since coming to Ashbaroth. He barely rose from his bed anymore. For two weeks now Eli hadn't seen him take up his needle and work at his canvas. He seemed to have lost all desire to do anything.

And it's all my fault, Eli thought morosely. *In Jerusalem, Father felt his work had a purpose. His one aim was to earn enough so that I could go to rabbinical school. Now he has lost his purpose. His will to work is gone as well. Ahead of him is nothing but sickness and death. And he would not hear of being healed by a miracle-worker!*

Chapter 4

"Simeon always hires more workers during the harvest," Joseph informed Eli as they set out for the fields. "You might see some you haven't met before."

Eli scanned the valley, his gaze stopping at a young man who was already busy, his sickle flashing as he cut bundles of grain. "Who is that?"

Joseph followed Eli's pointing finger, and his eyes widened. "Why, I do believe that is Asa, son of Simeon!"

"You mean the landowner's son? Why would he be working in the fields?" Eli asked in amazement.

Joseph shook his head. "I have no idea. I am as surprised as you are."

All morning Eli kept glancing at Asa. The young man's tunic was perhaps a little finer than the others', but he cut grain as well as the rest.

At lunchtime he will no doubt go up to his fine house to eat, Eli thought.

But when the other workers stopped to eat, Asa produced a scrip just like the others, a leather bag containing bread and cheese and parched grain.

You would never guess he is a rich man's son, Eli marveled.

One thing was different about Asa. When the talk turned to John the Baptist and Jesus, he did not join in. A pained expression crossed his face when there was coarse jesting about the wonders these men were reported to have done. Eli was equally withdrawn. He wished he could talk to Asa.

As it turned out, Asa wanted to talk to Eli.

"I have noticed you do not laugh mockingly when Jesus or John is discussed," Asa began guardedly the next day. His eyes searched Eli's face. "Does this mean—that you are a follower as well?"

"A follower? Of Jesus or John?" Eli said in amazement.

"Actually, I'm not a follower either," Asa whispered hastily. "That is, I haven't been baptized. But my father has received the baptism of John."

"Your father has?" Eli exclaimed. Eagerness surged through him. Perhaps Asa could answer some questions for him! "What does your father really believe about John? Is he a prophet? And what about Jesus? Do you intend to be baptized too?"

Smiling, Asa held up his free hand. "You are like a dam that has broken. You must have been bursting with questions!"

Eli felt his face grow warm. "It's just that my father has nothing good to say about these two men . . ." His voice trailed off. What if he frightened Asa by revealing this fact?

But Asa's smile did not waver. "My father is growing more and more interested in Jesus. John isn't baptizing much anymore, you see. He's like a man stepping down to let a better man take over. Do you know what John said about Jesus one day? 'He must increase, and I must decrease.' John compared himself to a friend of the bridegroom who rejoices when he hears the bridegroom's voice."

Eli's sickle paused in midair as he looked Asa full in the face. "So your father believes Jesus is . . . is the Messiah?" He could barely say the marvelous word.

"He doesn't know," Asa said, shaking his head.

Eli's heart fell. People were always saying they didn't know. He wanted to know, really know, who Jesus was!

Asa glanced around at the other workers. "Maybe we had better move apart if we don't want to be blamed for dawdling."

ONE EVENING SOON AFTERWARD, Uncle Shem came to visit at the House Ben Amos. The son of Father's father and his young second wife, Shem was only a few years older than Eli. Shem's mother was widowed now. She kept working to help support Shem's wife and two children, for Shem had a dream. It was the same dream Father had entertained for Eli: to become a learned rabbi. He studied each day under Zacharias, the village rabbi. Every now and then he went to Jerusalem to sit at the feet of the great teachers there. Father often spoke fondly of Shem. In him, at least, his dream might still come true.

This evening Shem was full of news from Jerusalem. "Nicodemus has had a talk with Jesus," he said as he sat on the floor near Father's pallet.

"Ah," said Father with satisfaction. "No doubt he gave that upstart something to think about."

Shem's eyes did not meet Father's. "I'm afraid the opposite is true."

"What do you mean?" Father demanded.

"Well, for one thing, Nicodemus went to see Jesus under cover of darkness." Shem shrugged. "I think he ought to have confronted the man openly. By going secretly he revealed his own confusion, don't you think?"

Father's eyes narrowed, but he refused to give an opinion. He would not easily think ill of the revered Nicodemus.

"Nicodemus called Jesus 'Rabbi' and suggested He must be a teacher sent from God," Shem went on. "I'm not sure why. He was flabbergasted when Jesus said something like, 'Verily I say unto you, except a man be born again, he cannot see the kingdom of God.' "

"Such talk," muttered Father.

Shem nodded in agreement. "Nicodemus asked how that could happen. How could a man enter a second time into his mother's womb?"

"A good comeback," Father said, chuckling. "I expect that stumped Jesus!"

"Not at all!" Shem replied, his face reddening with agitation. "If anything, Jesus took over after that! He said unless a man is born of water and the Spirit, he cannot enter into the kingdom of God. Jesus seemed to think Nicodemus should know what He was talking about! At one point He asked, 'Are you a ruler in Israel, and you don't know these things?' "

"What disrespect!" Father exclaimed indignantly.

"Nicodemus seems to have come under this man's spell," Shem went on regretfully. "If anything, he felt troubled that he knew so little of what Jesus was talking about. I think Nicodemus needs help fast. First thing we know . . ." Shem left the sentence dangling, but his gesture conveyed the meaning.

Eli, watching from his corner, thought wonderingly, *Why, Shem is suggesting that Nicodemus may be going crazy!*

Shem went on, his voice rising. "What Jesus said to Nicodemus amounts to blasphemy! He implies that He is the Son of God, that whoever believes on Him has everlasting life! And also, that anyone who does not believe is condemned!"

Eli felt a thrill in the very core of his being.

But not so his father. "Where is this blasphemer now?" he rasped.

"He went into the Judean wilderness. He has developed quite a following; they say that more are receiving His baptism than John's these days," Shem answered.

"So Jesus is baptizing too," Father muttered. "Ah, this is a dark time for Israel, when her people are being drawn away by blasphemers."

"I am sorry if I have disturbed you too much," said Shem, rising to his feet. "I will go now. I just felt it necessary for discerning wise men like you to hear about these things, in order to keep us from losing our way."

Eli glanced at Father. The wizened face glowed with pleasure; no doubt his brother's flattering words were a balm to his embittered soul.

As for Eli, his mind was whirling with excitement. He could hardly wait to tell Asa what he had heard! Next day they drew apart from the other workers to eat their lunch, and Eli began excitedly, "Guess what! It seems that even Nicodemus has been impressed by Jesus." He went on to tell his friend all he could remember of Uncle Shem's story.

Asa's eyes shone. "So Jesus Himself is claiming to be the Son of God! Last night my father told me something John said about Jesus." He paused, searching his memory. " 'He who is of the earth is earthly, and speaks of the earth; He who comes from heaven is above all, and testifies of what He has seen and heard... For He whom God has sent speaks the words of God.' "

Eli gazed at his friend ecstatically. "If this is true, then Jesus really is the Son of God, come to earth to tell us of the things He has seen in heaven!"

Asa nodded cautiously. "If it is true."

"I surely hope to hear this Jesus for myself someday," Eli declared.

"So do I," Asa answered.

Chapter 5

The month of Nisan drew to a close. Soon it was time for the Feast of the New Moon, to herald the month of Zif. Eli climbed to the housetop on the eve of the feast. Soon his mother joined him. "Are you hoping to see the signal fires?" she asked.

Eli gazed out over the darkening folds of the hills. "Do you think we can see any from this village? In Jerusalem we used to see them all the time." Tonight, according to tradition, watchmen would be set at certain high observation points around Jerusalem. At the first glimpse of the new moon, word was sent to the high priest, and the month would officially begin. Then signal fires were lit from hill to hill, passing word throughout the country. Though this ceremony was repeated at the beginning of every month, it never failed to stir Eli's excitement.

He got up and leaned over the parapet. "I can see a glow—over there toward Jerusalem. Yes, it's a signal fire!"

Mother scanned the sky. "I don't see the new moon."

"The watchers on their high points would see it

before we do," Eli reminded her.

Just then they heard a child crying. Mother started up, then chuckled. "I thought I recognized that cry," she said. "It's little Susanna. Uncle Shem must have brought his family to visit tonight." She hurried down the outside steps to the courtyard.

Eli followed her down apprehensively. What news was so important that Shem would come on the eve of the feast?

Awakened from his nap, Father smiled a welcome to his half brother. The baby had quieted down, and two-year-old Enoch was content to sit in his father's lap. "I have good news for you, Amos," Shem announced. "John the Baptist has finally been put into prison where he belongs."

Eli's knees suddenly felt weak, and he sat down quickly.

"Did our rulers convict John?" Father wondered.

"No. They didn't have to lift so much as a finger against him," came the reply. "John got himself into trouble. He had the audacity to rebuke Herod for taking his brother's wife, Herodias. She was so angry that she wanted John killed, but Herod couldn't bring himself to do it. So now John is in prison at Macheruous, near the Dead Sea, the loneliest place in the world, if you ask me."

Father sneered, "No doubt John will miss not being thronged by admiring followers any more."

Eli felt sick at heart. How could these two men talk that way about a humble, God-fearing man? He stole a glance at Ruth, Shem's wife. Did he see sadness on her face? Was she pained by her husband's attitude?

The next day, Eli lost no time in telling Asa the news. "I can't understand why God would allow this to happen to His prophet."

Asa mused sadly, "But haven't most of God's prophets through the ages been mistreated? And didn't John himself say that he must decrease, while Jesus must increase?"

"That's true," agreed Eli. Yet his heart felt heavy when he thought of John in that lonely prison down by the Dead Sea.

ONE BY ONE, the traditional "Seven Weeks of Harvest" slipped by. At the end of the seventh week, on the sixth of Sivan, came the Feast of Pentecost. "What does 'Pentecost' mean?" asked Isaac as Eli walked with Isaiah's family to the synagogue.

"Fiftieth," Eli answered promptly. "Because this is the fiftieth day after Passover. It's the anniversary of the giving of the Law to Moses at Mt. Sinai."

Isaiah reminded his young son, "This feast has other names besides Pentecost. It is called the Feast of Weeks, because we count seven weeks to time it. And because it comes at the end of the grain harvest, we also call it the Feast of Harvest."

When Isaiah paused, Joseph put in, "Don't forget, it's the Feast of Firstfruits too."

Isaac frowned. "Firstfruits? I thought we had that at Passover."

"That was only the meal offering from the first sheaf," Isaiah explained. "Now, at Pentecost, the first loaves made from the new grain are offered to the Lord."

"Pentecost is a pilgrimage festival and many people travel to Jerusalem. I wonder if Jesus will come?" Eli mused wistfully.

Joseph stared at him. "You act as though you wished to see Him!"

Eli did not reply. He wished he had not said that. It was clear that Joseph had no use for Jesus. As for Isaiah, Eli could not be sure. The older man wore a thoughtful look.

Once again it was Uncle Shem who brought news of Jesus to the House Ben Amos shortly after Pentecost. Shem had gone to Jerusalem for the feast. "I heard a good story about Jesus from some Galileans who were down for Pentecost," he said, smirking. "I think we can stop worrying about Jesus."

Alarm swept through Eli, who sat listening nearby. First John—then Jesus?

"Has He been assassinated?" Father questioned.

Shem chuckled. "No. Better than that. He has begun consorting with Samaritans."

Samaritans. The very word was evil for a good Jew. Jews didn't even say it unless they had to. Eli knew that a Jew who had anything to do with the Samaritans might as well be dead.

Situated between Galilee in the north and Judea in the south, Samaria was the most direct route for travelers between Galilee and Jerusalem. But good Jews never passed through Samaria on their journeys. They went down the mountains to the Jordan Valley and walked beside the river instead.

Eli was not sure why this hatred existed, except that there was something about the Samaritans being of mixed blood. He knew the Samaritans worshiped Jehovah, just like the Jews, but they had their own temple and their own priests. They also had their own Bible, which contained only the five books of Moses.

Shem took up his tale. "It seems this Jesus doesn't bother to take the river route on His journeys between Galilee and Judea. Instead He takes the ridge route—straight through Samaria."

Father nodded gravely. "Which proves He is just another careless Galilean with no regard for the holy Law."

Horror crept into Uncle Shem's voice as he went on, "And Jesus didn't just consort with your ordinary Samaritan either. He actually had a long chat with an immoral Samaritan woman—one who is known to have had a number of husbands!"

"Aaah." Father expelled a long sigh. "I must say I'm glad to know once and for all that Jesus is not a man of God. There were moments . . ." He hesitated, then confessed, "There were moments when I was starting to wonder."

Eli went up to bed later that night with mixed feelings. Part of him was happy because Father had admitted to being impressed with Jesus. Another part of him was bitter because Father only admitted it after he felt sure Jesus had made a mess of things. *Is consorting with Samaritans really so bad? Are they not just ordinary people who worship the same God as we do?* Eli wondered. The questions whirled endlessly in his mind.

Chapter 6

Sick as he was, Father rarely missed out on morning prayers. Sometimes Eli grew impatient as he huddled beneath his prayer shawl listening to the endless mumbling. He longed to be out and away to the fields. But morning prayers were very important to a Jew.

When prayers were over on the morning after Shem's visit, Father lifted his prayer shawl and remarked, "I don't suppose the rich man's son has showed up to help with the threshing."

"You mean Asa?" Eli shook his head sadly. "I haven't seen him since Pentecost."

Father smiled condescendingly. "Threshing is pretty hot, dusty work for one accustomed to a life of ease."

"Asa certainly did his part during harvest," Eli said defensively. He went to the other room to pick up his scrip, which Mother had filled with dry bread and parched grain. His heart felt heavy as he took the path down the valley. Had Father guessed right? Would Asa stop coming to help the workers now that they were threshing and winnowing the grain? How he longed to see his friend and talk to him about Uncle Shem's story of Jesus and the Samaritan woman!

Long before he reached the threshingfloor, Eli found himself peering intently at the workers pounding the grain with their flails. That one man there—he certainly looked like Asa. It was him! Eli fairly flew the rest of the way to the threshingfloor. Of course he could not speak to his friend now, but they sent each other big smiles that said, *See you at lunchtime.*

The other workers had come to accept that Eli and Asa drew apart to eat their lunch. Joseph Bar Isaiah had complained a few times, but when Eli invited him to join them, he refused.

"I missed you this past week," Eli said as he took a bite of his bread.

Asa nodded. "I should have told you about our plans. We were in Jerusalem for Pentecost, staying at my Uncle Benahab's."

"Was Jesus in Jerusalem for the feast?" Eli asked eagerly.

"Not that I know of. But we did hear an interesting story about Him, something that must have happened in the spring around Passover time. He was traveling through Samaria and stopped to rest at Jacob's well . . ."

"I wonder if this is the same story Uncle Shem was telling last night?" Eli broke in.

"So you know all about it. Wasn't that something, the way He offered living water to that woman?" Asa said.

"Living water?" Eli repeated blankly. "All I heard was that Jesus had a long chat with an immoral woman."

"Ah," said Asa knowingly. "A great deal depends on who is telling a story. We heard it from friends who have been baptized, and it is truly marvelous! Jesus asked this woman to give Him a drink. She was astonished that a Jew would do such a thing. Jesus said to her, 'If you knew who I am, you would ask Me to give you living water.' "

Eli drew his eyebrows together. "What did He mean?"

"Well, you see, Jesus was speaking of something spiritual. He told the woman to go and call her husband before He would give her of this living water. When the woman claimed she had no husband, Jesus told her the truth: 'You have had five husbands, and the one you have now is not your husband.' "

Eli smiled. "Uncle Shem said something about husbands. Was the woman offended at Jesus?"

Asa shook his head. "Not at all. She exclaimed, 'Sir, I perceive that You are a prophet!' Then she asked Him if the Jews were right in insisting that Jerusalem was the only proper place to worship." Asa paused. "The answer Jesus gave her is so marvelous, it took me awhile to understand what He meant. 'The hour is coming when the true worshipers shall worship neither in this mountain nor in Jerusalem, but in spirit and in truth. God is Spirit; those who worship Him must do it in spirit and in truth.' "

The strange words penetrated Eli's heart like a shaft of light. "In spirit and in truth," he mused. "That's revolutionary, isn't it, to suggest that Jerusalem may no longer be important in the future?"

Asa smiled. "I guess it is. This woman must have

been thinking along the same lines, because she started talking about the day Christ would come. And do you know what Jesus said? Plain as day, He told her, 'I who speak to you am He.' "

"He said that? He really did?" Eli said, his voice rising. Several men in the other group of workers glanced in their direction.

"Like you, that woman got pretty excited," Asa went on. "She ran home and set the whole town on fire with the news. The Samaritans begged Jesus to stay with them, and He began preaching—thus giving them the 'living water' He had promised. Many of them now believe that He is the Messiah."

"I wonder where Jesus is right now," Eli said, lowering his voice, though it still quivered with excitement.

"In Galilee, I'm told. But who knows? He might come to Jerusalem for our next pilgrimage festival—the Feast of Tabernacles in Tishri."

"That's still over three months away," Eli pointed out gloomily.

Asa was shading his eyes and staring up the hill. "I do believe that's Sharon, bringing us a fresh drink."

Stepping lightly down the path from the House Ben Simeon was a young girl clad in a simple white tunic and cloak. As she drew near Eli saw her shining black hair and large dark eyes. "One of your servants?"

Asa grinned. "No. My sister. So you haven't met Sharon?"

Eli shook his head, still watching the girl. She smiled shyly as she held out a jug to her brother.

Asa waved a hand. "Give Eli some first."

Eli was so astonished that he did not think to refuse. He took a long draught of the cool drink, then passed the jug to Asa, who thanked his sister as he handed it back. Her cloak swirled about her as she hurried back up the hill.

Impulsively, Eli turned to Asa. "There's something I've wanted to ask you for a long time. Why are you helping in your father's fields, mingling with us peasants? I'm sure you wouldn't have to work for a living."

"Because my father encouraged me to, and because I want to," Asa replied simply.

"But why?" Eli persisted.

Asa gave him a long look. "I'm surprised you haven't guessed. It's the influence of John and Jesus. Neither of them has any regard for high and low classes. Everybody is the same in the eyes of God."

Eli's heart warmed. No longer would he have to fear the loss of Asa's friendship. There were no barriers between them!

Chapter 7

Tammuz, the fourth month, brought with it the work of tending the grapevines. Asa and Eli often contrived to work side by side on the terraces, pruning and training the vines so that the bunches of grapes would receive maximum exposure to the sun. There on the sunny hillside, Eli heard many stories about Jesus from Asa. He heard how Jesus healed a nobleman's son in Capernaum without even going to see the sick boy. And he heard about Jesus' visit to His hometown of Nazareth, where He spoke in the synagogue and told His former neighbors that His coming heralded God's Year of Jubilee.

While Asa was telling about this, Eli remarked, "Those Nazarenes who had only known Jesus as a carpenter must have been really impressed!"

But Asa shook his head. "I'm afraid not. Father says the people of Nazareth were so offended they took Jesus to the top of a hill, intending to throw Him to His death!"

Eli shuddered. "How could they do that?"

"They couldn't, that's what," Asa said with a smile.

"Jesus slipped quietly out of their hands and escaped."

Eli shook his head slowly. "Such amazing things you tell me. How does your father find out these things?"

"He goes to Jerusalem often. Then, too, he has friends in Galilee who send letters." Asa paused. "Father wants to invite some of the villagers for a Sabbath meal. Do you think you could come? And your parents too? He spoke of asking the House Ben Isaiah as well."

"I would like that very much," Eli responded, "but I doubt if Father would come. He's ashamed to be seen being carried around on a pallet."

"I suspect he doesn't like my father very well either," Asa said shrewdly.

Eli felt his face grow warm. "He should, since we earn our bread in your fields. But he . . . he is a proud man."

Asa nodded. "I thought as much. What of the House Ben Isaiah? Do you think they will come?"

Eli thought for a moment. "I believe the parents would, and I'm sure Isaac would be delighted. I don't know much about Hannah, though I think she'd go wherever her parents do. As for Joseph . . . he doesn't seem to appreciate the teachings of John or Jesus very much."

"I know. He often joins in the mocking," Asa agreed. "I hope you can come next Sabbath, then."

"I only hope my father won't prevent me from coming," Eli said, frowning.

That very evening, as Father lay napping, Eli went to his mother. "Asa Bar Simeon has invited us to their house for a Sabbath meal," he said.

She looked up from the pot she was stirring. Amazement flooded her face. Eli could imagine what she was thinking—that a common working-class family should be invited to the house of a rich man! After a moment she shook her head. "Father will not want to go."

"But I? May I go without you? The House Ben Isaiah is invited too."

She stared at him for a long moment. "I don't see why you shouldn't go."

"Will it be all right with Father?"

She smiled. "You are a man, able to make your own decisions. Old enough to be betrothed, even married."

The unexpected words left Eli speechless with confusion. How could she have guessed that whenever he thought of visiting the House Ben Simeon, a picture floated into his mind of a dark-haired girl tripping lightly up the hillside with her jug? But it was preposterous that he should be thinking about a rich man's daughter. For one thing, how could he ever pay the dowry?

Surely Mother would not dream of such a thing. If she did, she said nothing of it. Instead she asked, "You are hoping to hear more about Jesus if you go there?"

Eli stared at her. "Who told you that Simeon is—I mean, that he takes a great interest in the doings of Jesus?"

"I go to the well to draw water," she replied with a smile. "So do dozens of other village women. Women talk, you know." She lowered her voice. "I hope you hear more about Jesus, and tell me what you learn."

"Oh, Mother," he said, his voice quivering, "I didn't know you—well, I thought maybe you shared Father's hatred of Jesus and John."

She shook her head. "Perhaps I did, at first. But the things I hear are so marvelous . . ." A sound from the inner room brought her swiftly to her feet. "I must see what Father wants," she said, hurrying away.

LEAVING BEHIND the narrow streets and poor dwellings in the poorer section of Ashbaroth, Eli and the family of Isaiah walked up the hill toward the grand homes of the rich. "I have never been in this part of town before," Isaac told Eli. "Why, those houses must be three stories high!"

"I feel out of place," Eli admitted just as Isaiah stopped in front of a magnificent house. "Is this where Simeon lives? I only see the back of their home from the fields." He gazed at the spacious courtyard with its stately trees and the tall columns on either side of the great door.

The door opened. Simeon stepped out, welcomed them warmly, and invited them inside. Eli caught his breath at the rich brocade hangings and the gilded cushions on the bench running around the walls. Through an open doorway he saw a table, spread with a gleaming cloth and surrounded by couches for the diners to recline upon.

Eli glanced down at his large, calloused hands. Would his table manners be good enough for such sur-roundings? The fact that Simeon's four daughters joined them at the table did not ease his nervousness. And how strange it was to have servants wash his feet!

Since it was the Sabbath, all the food had been prepared beforehand and there was no hot soup. Everything was of such a fine quality that Eli could not stop being amazed at finding himself in such a place.

The men were soon talking about Jesus. From Isaiah's earnest questions, Eli could see that his interest was heartfelt and sincere. He listened, enthralled, as Simeon told of Jesus' growing fame. Everywhere He went, in the villages and towns of Galilee, great crowds followed Him with their lame and blind and sick to seek healing.

"And He heals them all?" Eli found himself asking.

Simeon nodded. "Even the lepers and those with palsy. One story told to me shows that the Master even knows what people are thinking."

The Master. Several times today Eli had heard Simeon calling Jesus the Master. What a marvelous thing, that even a rich man who had never seen this lowly preacher should call Him Master!

"Will you tell us the story you referred to?" Isaiah prompted.

Simeon nodded. "Jesus was sitting in a house in Capernaum, preaching to a crowd that spilled out into the streets. Some friends of a sick man had carried him to the place on his pallet but were unable to get through the door. So they opened a hole in the roof over Jesus' head and let down the pallet at His feet!"

"They must have been very sure Jesus could cure the man," Asa observed.

Simeon nodded again. "Faith. They had lots of faith in the power of Jesus. But Jesus' first words were, 'My son, your sins are forgiven you.' Now there were some Pharisees standing nearby . . ." Simeon paused and looked at Eli, his eyes twinkling. "I hope you won't be offended."

Eli chuckled. "You mean because I am the son of a Pharisee? Don't worry."

Simeon smiled, then continued, "Jesus looked at those Pharisees and said, 'I know what is in your hearts. You are thinking that I am wicked to say such a thing, for only God has the power to forgive sins. But which is easier to say: "Your sins are forgiven" or, "Rise up and walk"?'

"Then Jesus turned to the man with palsy and told him to take his bed and go home." Simeon's eyes glowed as he looked around the table. "And that is just what the man did."

"I wonder how the Pharisees felt then," Isaiah mused.

Simeon smiled sadly. "Sometimes it seems that those refusing to believe in the Master's power are filled with violent hatred."

Eli swallowed hard, thinking of his father lying ill and bitter at home. "I don't suppose Jesus could heal people who are like that."

"I think not," said Simeon kindly. He knew about Amos. "Faith comes before healing."

A dream died for Eli. Sometimes he had imagined Jesus coming to Ashbaroth, and he asking Him to come to the House Ben Amos. "My father is against you," he had pictured himself saying to the Master. "But if You would heal him, he would surely believe in You then."

Eli knew now such a thing was not possible. His shoulders drooped and his steps lagged as he walked home with the others.

Isaiah noticed Eli's mood. "It is hard when a family is divided because of Jesus," he said sympathetically.

Then Eli remembered—Joseph had not been with his parents today. The House Ben Isaiah was divided as well.

Chapter 8

After the month of Ab came Elul, the time of grape harvest. Asa and Eli were busy picking the luscious bunches of fruit into large, straw baskets. These were loaded onto donkeys, one huge basket slung on either side of the patient beasts. Other workers led the donkeys down to the wine press where men trod upon the grapes in huge stone vats to press out the sweet juice.

"Father would like you and the family of Isaiah to come for another Sabbath meal," Asa told Eli while they picked grapes one day.

Eli looked up, surprised. "I will gladly come. Probably Isaiah will too."

"What about Hannah, daughter of Isaiah? Will she come again, do you think?" Asa asked shyly.

Eli stared at him. A slow smile came to his lips. That Asa should have noticed Hannah was something Eli had never dreamed. Hannah was a plain, quiet girl who reminded Eli of a shy mouse. "So you want to see Hannah again," he said.

Asa's face was crimson. "I should like to, yes. She is a very nice girl, wouldn't you say?"

"Why, yes . . ." Eli's voice trailed off lamely.

"But not as nice as my sister Sharon?" Asa asked shrewdly.

Now it was Eli's turn to feel his face grow warm. How could Asa have guessed?

As though in answer to Eli's unspoken question, Asa said, "I am not blind. And Sharon has mentioned you."

"Do you mean . . ." Eli sputtered.

"I wouldn't say it if it weren't so," Asa replied.

Eli had a wonderful secret to be held close and told to no one, not even his mother, who was glad to hear that he would go and find out more about Jesus.

After the second visit to the House Ben Simeon, Eli told his mother how Jesus had chosen twelve men to be His helpers, how He had caused a fisherman's net to overflow with fish, and how He had healed a leper.

The month fled by, until it was the eve of the Feast of Trumpets, which would usher in the month of Tishri. "It will be strange not to be awakened by the temple trumpets tomorrow morning," Eli remarked to his mother as he went up to bed.

"Will there be no trumpets here in Ashbaroth?" she wondered.

"Perhaps a few, but nothing like the trumpets of Jerusalem, I'm sure," Eli replied. He went to sleep dreaming of the shofar's silvery notes calling, calling from the ramparts of the temple.

Sometime after midnight Eli was roused by a strange noise downstairs. He sat up on the goatskin that served as his bed, straining to listen.

There it was again, an eerie, half-strangled moan. Eli had never heard anything like it. It must be Father. He pulled on his tunic and scrambled down the ladder. "Mother, what is wrong?"

"Please come," she answered, her voice carrying a note of fear.

She was huddled by Father's pallet, her hands fastened around his wrists, trying to restrain him. Father's body writhed as though in torture. "His legs. Try to keep him from thrashing so," she instructed Eli tensely.

Eli grabbed the flailing ankles, but they jerked from his hands. Where did all this strength come from? Wasn't Father weak and ill? Fear coursed through Eli, robbing him of his own strength. "Hadn't I better go for help?"

Mother did not look up. "We have no money for a doctor."

"Well, then, Isaiah, or Uncle Shem, or somebody?" he pleaded.

Mother lifted her face, and Eli saw a look of firm determination mixed with stark despair. "Eli, your father has had these spells before. There is nothing we can do about it."

He stared. "You mean this is not the first time?"

She shook her head. "They've been coming ever since he's bedridden. This is the worst one yet."

"And you never told me?" Eli reproached her.

She stroked Father's sweaty forehead. The moans and the writhing had subsided. "There was no need . . . no need for you to . . . to bear the shame."

Father's eyes were still glazed in unconsciousness. Eli protested, "Why shame? Is illness shameful?"

Mother did not look up. "You don't understand."

"Well, then, help me understand!" he pleaded.

She shook her head. "Please, just believe me. We cannot ask others for help. We must manage alone."

Eli slumped at the foot of the bed. "I don't understand, but I'll obey."

Her voice brightened. "This is a feast day, and you will not be working. Can you stay here with me? Father is often weak after a such a spell, needing help with everything."

"Sure," said Eli, hiding his disappointment. He had looked forward to going to the synagogue. "Does Father remember these spells?"

"I never tell him."

When he awoke at dawn, Father seemed confused. His rambling speech terrified Eli. Yet by midmorning his mind had cleared again, and he was calm the rest of the day. Isaiah came over to visit in the afternoon, along with Joseph and Isaac. The three boys climbed to the housetop.

"Did you hear the trumpets this morning, Eli?" Isaac asked.

"Yes, I did. They were not as loud as the ones at the temple on this feast, though. There, as soon as one trumpet is silent, another takes over, so that the sound carries on and on," Eli told him.

"Because it's the Seventh New Moon, of course. You knew that, didn't you?" Joseph shot back.

"Well, yes, but why do we call it the Seventh New Moon, when it's also the beginning of the New Year?" Isaac persisted.

Eli answered quickly, to ward off Joseph's

impatience. "Because we Jews celebrate two New Years in twelve months' time. When God gave Moses the observance of the Passover, He said that Nisan is to be the beginning of months. So Nisan marks the beginning of our sacred year, and it is the month from which we count the New Moons. That is why Tishri is the seventh." He paused for breath. "But our civil year, the year of farming, starts now in the Seventh New Moon! I'm sure you can understand why. Tishri is the month when the harvest is over and the farmer begins plowing and sowing."

Isaac frowned in concentration. "So this might be called our Second New Year?"

Eli chuckled. "If you like. Some people believe it's the anniversary of the beginning of the world too."

"I doubt if they know," Joseph put in skeptically.

"Maybe not," Eli conceded. "Maybe they don't know about this being the Day of Judgment either."

"Oh, yes, I believe that," Joseph was quick to say. "Grandfather says that on the New Year all God's people pass before His eyes like a flock of sheep before a shepherd, and God examines them all."

"Quite a task, if you ask me," murmured Eli. *What does God see when He looks at me?* he wondered inwardly. *Somebody confused, I think.*

Isaac had still more questions. "But why do the trumpets keep on blowing today?"

"Why, it's to remind God to remember His people and to remind them to call on Him for the promised blessings in the fulfillment of the covenant," Joseph replied.

The words echoed in Eli's mind. *"Fulfillment of the covenant." Has that time come at last? Is Jesus the One sent to fulfill God's covenant with Israel? But why are so many opposed to Him?*

Isaac prattled on, "And how many sacrifices will there be at the temple today?"

"Oh, quite a few," answered Eli. "There'll be the regular morning and evening sacrifices of a lamb; then the usual New Moon offerings, which I think consist of two bullocks, one ram, and seven lambs; and then, because it's the Seventh New Moon, there will be another festive offering of one bullock, one ram, seven lambs, and one goat for a sin offering."

Isaac gave a little shudder. "All those animals getting killed just because it's the New Year!" He thought for a moment. "But why do we need a sin offering today? I thought that is done once a year, on the tenth of this month, the Day of Atonement?"

Eli tweaked the little boy's ear. "You seem to know a lot about the sacrificial laws, Isaac. We need more than one sacrifice for sin in a year's time, you see, because we sin too often."

"Do we? Are we bad?" Isaac was perplexed.

Joseph gave Eli a wry smile. "You got yourself into this," he said. "You know how Isaac is with his questions."

Eli bent down until his eyes were even with Isaac's. "It's true. No matter how hard we try, we always sin again."

This silenced Isaac for a minute. Then he asked a mind-boggler. "If we have to make offerings for sin all the time anyway, why bother to try to be good?"

"Oh, Isaac!" chuckled Joseph. "You ask questions that have no answers."

Eli was silent. Were there really no answers? Did God want people to be in the dark about these things? Or was it possible, as Simeon seemed to believe, that God was about to reveal His will in a clear new way through Jesus?

Chapter 9

On the morning after the Feast of Trumpets, Father was still very weak but Mother encouraged Eli to go to work. "You know we need the money," she said.

Eli spent the week picking olives and carrying them to the great stone olive press where the oil was extracted. He had hoped to go to the synagogue on the Day of Atonement, because it is one of the most important days in the Jewish calendar. But it was not to be. Father was worse again, and Mother gratefully accepted Eli's offer to stay at home.

Asa had great plans for the weeklong Feast of Tabernacles, which began on the fifteenth. "I'm going to Jerusalem. Why don't you come along?" he proposed as he and Eli picked olives.

"I wish I could!" Eli said enthusiastically. "We could watch for Jesus!" Then he shook his head slowly. "But I know I can't go. Mother needs me, now that Father is worse."

"That's too bad," Asa said regretfully. "Couldn't someone else stay with your parents?"

Eli shook his head again. "Mother is so proud; she

does not like accepting help from others." He longed to tell his friend about Father's frightening spells. "But I hope you go to Jerusalem. And if you see Jesus, you can tell me all about Him."

"I'll gladly do that," Asa agreed. "Will you bother with a booth if your father can't use it?"

"I doubt it. Somehow I haven't the heart for all these old customs anymore," Eli confessed.

"You sound like my father. He isn't building a booth either. He says the teachings of the Master are influencing him away from such things."

Eli decided he would not even tell Mother about the opportunity to go with his friend to Jerusalem for fear she would want him to go. He didn't want to leave her alone with Father.

Once again, Isaiah and his family showed their concern for the sick man by coming to visit on the first day of the Feast of Tabernacles. Joseph looked around the courtyard after his father had gone inside. "I see you don't have a booth either."

"You don't either?" Eli questioned.

"No, but I wish we had built one," Joseph said unhappily. "We are not obeying the Law. The Law says Israelites are to dwell in booths for seven days as a reminder that the children of Israel lived in booths when they were delivered from Egypt."

Eli was silent, remembering the booths he and his father had built other years. Vendors hawked tree branches on the street corners in Jerusalem, and he and Father would go out and buy enough to build a shelter. There they would eat and sleep throughout that week. For a young boy, it was a fine adventure.

That week had never seemed too long for him!

This year, however, the week dragged on endlessly. He could hardly wait to hear all his friend would have to tell when he came home! Asa still had not returned when Eli went back to work after the feast. For two days he remained in suspense while plowing the tortuous hills and valleys of Simeon's land.

On the third day he spied another yoke of oxen toiling in the distance. Could that be Asa? He watched eagerly as the ponderous beasts drew near. Yes, the plowman was his friend! Once the two friends came alongside each other, the oxen had a good long rest.

"I did a lot of exploring, but I didn't see the Master," said Asa. "I doubt if He was in Jerusalem. I even visited the pool of Bethesda. They say that Bethesda means 'House of Mercy,' but when I saw all those sick and lame people lying in the porches around the pool, I wondered why the place has such a name."

"I've been there," Eli said, nodding. "But isn't it true that an angel stirs the water at certain times, and whoever steps into the water first can be healed?"

"So it is said, but the angel must not come very often. During warm weather the place is very crowded."

"What if Jesus were to come there someday?" Eli exclaimed.

"Ah, that would be a great sight," mused Asa. "Imagine Him healing all those people, perhaps with a single word!"

"I wonder if He will ever come back to Jerusalem," Eli said wistfully.

"He was here for the Passover last spring," Asa

reminded him. "Next year's Passover is only a few months away now." He glanced at his oxen, standing patiently in the furrow. "I should get going, but I just remembered something else I heard about Jesus. They say He can even cast evil spirits out of the demon-possessed!"

Eli stared at him. The words *evil spirits* struck him like a bolt of lightning.

"What's the matter?" Asa asked curiously when Eli continued to stare, as though his mind were elsewhere.

"Oh, I was just thinking," Eli said quickly. "A person possessed by a demon couldn't have faith in the Master's power, could he?"

"I guess the one who brings him to Jesus would have to have faith," Asa said after a thoughtful pause.

Eli spoke to his oxen, and they lurched forward, dragging the plowshare through the hard soil. For the rest of the day, his mind was in a whirl. Was Father demon-possessed? That would explain why Mother was ashamed. Why had he not thought of it before?

Despite this new and terrible realization about Father's illness, Eli's heart sang. There was hope for Father, if Jesus had power over evil spirits! Even if Father had no faith, he could be cured—if his son provided the faith. *Will I have the courage to tell this to Mother?* Eli wondered.

Surprisingly, it was Mother who first brought up the subject. Father was napping when Eli came home, so they waited for him to wake before starting supper.

"Uncle Shem was here today," Mother said. "He was angry and got Father quite worked up. Shem said the Pharisees heard that Jesus drove an evil spirit out of a man. They are indignant because Jesus did it on a Sabbath day, and right in a synagogue at that. Shem says it proves all the more that Jesus is not a man of God!"

Eli was thoughtful. "But, Mother," he said quietly, "if the Pharisees don't believe Jesus is a man of God, where do they think He receives the power to drive out an evil spirit?"

"They think He does it by the power of the Evil One himself."

Eli shuddered. "Do you believe that?"

She looked up, perplexed. "I don't know. I think not."

"I would far rather believe His power is from God," Eli stated. "Believing is so important, Mother," he rushed on. "Only those who believe in Jesus can be healed, you see."

"Believe in Jesus? I'm not sure what you mean."

Eli explained carefully, "People who want to be healed have to believe He has the power to do it. But in the case of one who is demon-possessed, such a person wouldn't be able to believe. So the one who brings the victim to Jesus—the parents, or children, or whoever—must have faith in the Master's power."

Mother's eyes widened. "That sounds preposterous," she muttered, turning abruptly toward the inner room.

Eli held his cold hands over the brazier. He was still unsure about Father being possessed by a demon. Had Mother guessed what he was thinking?

One thing was obvious: she was not comfortable with the idea of the Master coming to heal Father.

Chapter 10

In spite of the chilly, damp winter, Father's condition kept improving. It had been so long since he had had a spell that Eli dared ask his mother whether he could visit the House Ben Simeon again.

"May I go up to the House Ben Simeon during the Festival of Lights?" he asked. "We're invited to enjoy the feast with them."

Mother quickly agreed. "You deserve to get away sometimes."

"I wish you could go too," Eli told her.

She shook her head. "I find fulfillment in caring for your father."

So it came about on the 25th of Kislev that Eli walked up the hill with the family of Isaiah, all except for Joseph.

"You promised to tell us why this is sometimes called the Festival of Lights and sometimes the Feast of Dedication," Isaac reminded his father.

Isaiah smiled indulgently. "Well, about 200 years ago, Judea was not under the rule of Rome as it is now. Instead it was held by Antiochus IV, an evil Syrian ruler who caused much destruction and bloodshed. One day a false rumor started, claiming that Antiochus was dead. Great rejoicing broke out in Judea! But Antiochus was not dead at all, and the rejoicing of the people infuriated him. Soon the joy was turned into mourning as the Syrian army took Jerusalem by storm and killed tens of thousands. Many thousands more were sold as slaves."

Isaac—who had probably heard this story many times before—was nevertheless wide-eyed. "Were there any Jews left after that?"

"Oh, yes," Isaiah assured him. "But not many happy Jews, I think. For the Syrians went right into the temple and offered a sow on the altar of burnt offerings."

"A pig—in the temple!" Like any Jewish boy, Isaac realized how blasphemous it would be for an unclean animal to be in the sanctuary.

Isaiah nodded soberly. "As if that weren't bad enough, they made a broth of the sow's flesh and sprinkled it about, until the temple was utterly defiled. For three years after that, foreign Syrian gods were worshiped in Zion."

Eli glanced at Isaac. His serious young face showed horror.

"However," Isaiah continued on a brighter note, "the Jews did not just stand by helplessly. They organized an army under the leadership of Judas Maccabaeas. Remember what that name means?"

Isaac grinned. "Judas 'the Hammer.' "

"Right. Maccabaeas and his army hammered the enemy who had taken over their land. Finally, in a fierce battle near Jerusalem, the Maccabeans were victorious. 'Behold, our enemies are crushed,' declared Judas. 'Let us go up and cleanse the sanctuary and dedicate it again to the Lord.' This happened on the 25th of Kislev. That explains why it's called the Feast of Dedication.

"Now the name 'Feast of Lights' is based on a tradition that only one cruse of holy oil could be found in the temple after the Syrian idols had been thrown out. It is said that this oil miraculously lasted for eight days. That is why so many lamps are burned at the temple this week, in honor of that miraculous cruse of oil."

They walked in silence.

"I wish we had a Judas Maccabaeas today to free us from the Romans," exclaimed Isaac.

Isaiah shook his head. "Different men have tried to be a 'Maccabee' over the years, but the Roman 'hammer' always pounds them into the dust."

"What about Jesus, the Galilean Rabbi?" Isaac questioned.

His whole family stared at him in astonishment, but the boy persisted, "Crowds of people follow Jesus. Couldn't He organize an army to free us from the Romans?"

Isaiah's reply startled Eli. "Perhaps He could, Isaac. He will do it in His own good time."

Eli was excited. The thought had occurred to him before, but he had cast it aside as impossible. What could a lowly Rabbi from Galilee do against a mighty Roman army? But if Isaiah thought it was possible, then perhaps it was. Scriptures did speak of the Messiah as being the Deliverer!

It was Isaac's mother, Leah, who now spoke reproachfully, "We shouldn't give the boy ideas. The last thing our land needs is another uprising, with thousands getting killed."

"The trouble is, people don't wait for God's timing," Isaiah answered quietly.

They reached the House Ben Simeon, and the door was thrown open in welcome. It was a day of good fellowship and good food, a refreshing oasis in the midst of Eli's hardworking days.

When it was time to go home, Asa urged his sisters, "Let's walk with them for a short way!" It was soon obvious what he had in mind, for he and Hannah lagged a few steps behind the rest, talking in low tones. For a moment Eli wondered what it might be like if he did the same with Sharon, but he didn't dare. His father's disapproval stood between them like a high wall.

"Have you seen the temple during the Festival of Lights?" Isaac asked, breaking into Eli's brooding thoughts.

When Eli nodded, Isaac begged, "Tell me what it's like!"

"Well, there are lights everywhere, in the Outer Court and the Court of the Women and the Court of the Israelites. Every day more lamps are lit, until you are almost blinded by the dazzling light. People joyfully celebrate the time when the temple was rededicated to the worship of Jehovah. The courts are filled with people singing the Great Hallel—[Psalms 120–136] and waving palm branches."

"I wish I could see it someday," Isaac remarked.

"You know," Isaiah observed, "I have been thinking of some words from the Great Hallel: 'God is the Lord, which hath shewed us light.' Do not the Scriptures say that God is the light of the world? He is greater than all the lights in the temple."

The girls began to sing the Great Hallel. Eli listened for a moment before he, too, joined in. Sharon's dark eyes shone as her silvery voice rang out.

Sharon's face stayed in Eli's mind, even after he entered his own home, which suddenly seemed very small and poor compared to the House Ben Simeon.

"You are spending a lot of time up on the hill these days," Father commented sarcastically as they ate the evening meal together.

Eli was silent, stung by the injustice. This was the first time in over a month that he had visited Asa's family.

"I hope you don't start getting vain ideas from associating with a rich Sadducee," Father warned.

Eli nodded mutely, though his mind seethed. Would Father forbid him the only pleasure he had in life?

But the crippled man fell silent as he struggled to bring his sop to his mouth with twisted fingers. Later, alone on the housetop, Eli allowed himself to think about Sharon again. *But what is the use?* he asked himself in frustration. *Father will never consent to our betrothal. His narrow-mindedness is like a chain wrapped around me. He is chained to the Law, and I am chained to him.*

What Asa told him the next day only fueled Eli's bitterness. They were working side by side at one of the lowliest tasks, cleaning out irrigation ditches. Rich man's son though he was, Asa could sling shovels full of mud just as fast as Eli. He leaned on his shovel for a moment, eyes shining. "I am going to ask Isaiah for Hannah's hand in marriage," he said.

The words were not unexpected, yet Eli's mind had to adjust to the thought. "I am glad for you," he managed to say.

Asa gazed thoughtfully at him. "What about you? Have you been thinking about betrothal?"

"I . . . I wish you wouldn't ask," Eli admitted, his voice rough with emotion.

"I hope you realize that my father would not be opposed, if . . . if . . . well, you did admit once that you are attracted to Sharon."

"But what good would it do to let myself think such things? My father would be dead against it," Eli almost shouted as his frustration brimmed up and engulfed him.

"I'm sorry," Asa said quietly. He bent to his shoveling, then repeated, "I'm sorry. I didn't want to hurt you. I didn't realize . . ."

"No, you have no idea what my life is like," Eli agreed grimly. "You can't imagine how . . ." Eli's voice trailed off in despair.

But he could not stop thinking about Sharon. What if she and he would go away somewhere, away from Father's iron hand? They could get married and travel up to Galilee, where they could sit at the Master's feet and learn from Him every day.

Chapter 11

The rainy winter months slipped by while the barley and the wheat steadily grew and ripened. Finally it was Nisan again, the "beginning of months" according to the Law. Once again Asa went up to Jerusalem for the Passover. Once again Eli awaited his return with feverish anticipation. Surely this time Asa would see Jesus!

One morning Asa was back among the workers cutting barley. At noon he and Eli carried their lunches to the grove, away from the others.

"You've seen Him!" cried Eli, looking into Asa's face. "I can tell by the way your eyes are shining."

"I almost saw Him," Asa admitted with a twinge of regret. "I kept asking if anyone had seen Jesus, but nobody seemed to know whether He was in Jerusalem for the feast or not. I decided to visit Bethesda one day, and I arrived just after something wonderful had happened. Jesus had just been there, and He had healed a man who had been crippled for thirty-eight years! I just missed it."

"Amazing!" Eli exclaimed. "I wonder why He singled out only one man to heal? There must have been dozens of others there."

"I wondered too," Asa admitted. "But I wasn't going to let it bother me. I still can't believe I almost saw Jesus, and performing a miracle at that!"

"That would have been a privilege indeed," Eli agreed as he closed his scrip and got to his feet. During the afternoon he dreamed once more how it would be if Jesus would come to Ashbaroth. By evening he was so filled with the idea that he told Mother about the healing at Bethesda and added impulsively, "What if Jesus were to come here and heal Father?"

Mother was startled. For a moment her eyes brightened, but then they clouded again. "Father would never consent to it," she said.

Eli's shoulders slumped. "Why are the Pharisees so set against Jesus, anyway?"

"A lot of it is because Jesus seems to disregard our laws," Mother pointed out. "Didn't you say it was the Sabbath when Jesus bade that cripple to pick up his bed and walk?"

Eli groaned. "So you think the Pharisees would look right past the miracle and make a fuss about a man carrying his bed on the Sabbath?"

Mother was only too right, as Uncle Shem proved a few days later.

"Have you heard that the rabble-rouser from Galilee is back in Jerusalem?" he snapped to Father. "He is encouraging our people to desecrate the Sabbath!"

Father's withered hands clenched into fists. "No. I hadn't heard."

So Mother didn't tell him about the miracle at Bethesda? Eli thought in surprise.

Uncle Shem told Father in great detail how Jesus

had told the man to carry his bed on the Sabbath.

"Now what?" Father rasped. "What are our rulers going to do about this man?"

Shem looked around importantly. "Our minds have been made up for us. This blasphemer must die."

Eli gasped. He wanted to leap up and protest, "You can't do that! Jesus is a Man sent from God!" But he sat frozen on the floor near Father's pallet.

"You see," Uncle Shem went on, "it's not just the breaking of the Sabbath. Some of the Sanhedrin interviewed Jesus." He hesitated, then admitted, "Well, I guess Jesus did most of the talking. His claims are impossible. He calls God His own Father, making Himself equal with God! What's more, He claims to be able to give life to people who have died. And while He speaks so highly of Himself, He grinds our respected leaders into the dust. During the interview, He charged them, 'You do not have the love of God in yourselves!' "

Shem got up and paced restlessly around the room. "So you see, He condemns Himself with His own words."

"Why have they not already taken Him?" accused Father.

Shem held up his hands as though shielding himself from blame. "I wasn't there. I don't know what they're waiting for."

They may not find it so easy to take this Man captive, Eli thought, remembering how Jesus had slipped away from His tormentors in Nazareth last year.

ASA POURED OUT a basket of grain and watched the chaff float away on the breeze. In a guarded whisper he confided to Eli, "We know where Jesus is now."

"You do!" exclaimed Eli. News about Jesus had been sparse ever since His brief appearance in Jerusalem during the Passover.

"He's back in Galilee," Asa went on, glancing at his friend. "You look disappointed."

"Galilee is a long way from here," Eli said.

"With our rulers seeking to kill Him, Jesus is better off far away," Asa reminded him. "But let me tell you something more. John the Baptist has sent some of his disciples to Galilee with a message for Jesus. They are to ask Jesus if He is really the Messiah who is to come, or do we look for another."

Eli's flail hung motionless. "You mean John doubts that Jesus is the Messiah? He was pretty sure about it when he was preaching!"

"I would get discouraged too, if I were shut up in that awful prison down by Machaerus," Asa responded. "In fact, I've sometimes wondered why Jesus doesn't exert His power to set John free."

Eli thought that over. "He could probably do it. Isn't the Messiah supposed to be the Deliverer? Maybe John is wondering when Jesus will rise up and free us from the Romans!"

"Maybe so. But Jesus doesn't keep company with the kind of people who would make good soldiers. We hear He eats with tax collectors and sinners."

"Tax collectors!" Eli shuddered. "I don't understand what Jesus sees in those people."

Asa gave him a reproachful look. "You're as bad as the Pharisees. They once asked the Rabbi's disciples why their Master sat at table with those people. Jesus told the Pharisees that those who are well don't need a doctor; He has come to save those who know they need help, not those who think they are good enough!"

Eli felt his face grow warm. "I'd rather be one who realizes his need, than to be like the Pharisees. They are too sure of their own righteousness."

Asa gazed up into the surrounding hills. "Sometimes I wonder just what true righteousness is, anyway."

"Questions, questions," said Eli with a wry smile. "It seems we have nothing but questions. And now you say even John the Baptist is questioning Jesus. I'm beginning to feel discouraged."

"Who knows? Perhaps we will be greatly encouraged by the Master's reply to John's messengers," Asa countered. "My father is starting off today to visit John in prison, and when he returns, he will know the outcome. He said to invite our friends for another Sabbath meal. I hope you can come."

"I don't see why not," Eli said eagerly.

A week later found Eli at the table in the House Ben Simeon with Isaiah's family. Simeon was soon talking about his trip to Machaerus.

"John's messengers to Jesus were back," Simeon said. "Jesus didn't actually say He was the Christ. But He told them to tell John about all the wonderful things He was doing. And Jesus plainly said John the Baptist is the one of whom it is written, 'Behold, I send My messenger before your face, who shall prepare your way before you.'"

A soft voice spoke from the corner where the women sat. "So if John was the messenger, Jesus must be the Messiah."

Without turning to look, Eli knew it was Sharon

who had spoken. Her voice had rung with conviction. Sharon was not like him, wanting to believe that Jesus was the Christ, yet still waiting to be convinced.

"Jesus speaks of the kingdom of heaven," Asa said. "Does that mean His own kingdom? Why does He stay in the backwaters of Galilee if He is actually a King?"

"I can understand why you're impatient," Simeon answered with a gentle smile. "Sometimes I feel the same way. But we must remember Jesus has a different view than we do. He doesn't keep company with those who consider themselves wise and great. Once He prayed aloud among a crowd of poor people, 'Father, I praise You that You have hidden these things from the wise and intelligent, and revealed them to babes.' "

Isaiah nodded slowly. "That's the trouble with so many in Israel. They are too snobbish to receive One who comes in a lowly manner."

"Jesus longs to help the poor and needy," Simeon went on. " 'Come to Me,' He invited the crowd, 'all who labor and are burdened, and I will give you rest.' "

The words struck a chord in Eli's heart. Rest! To have rest from the burdens and conflicts within! The solution, it seemed, was simple: come to Jesus. *But how,* Eli asked himself, *how am I to come to Jesus? He is in Galilee, and I am in Ashbaroth of Judea.*

Chapter 12

Uncle Shem brought the tragic news to the House Ben Amos one evening after supper. Following his customary greetings to Father, he announced abruptly, "John is dead."

Eli drew in his breath sharply. Behind him he heard Mother's gasp.

Father was startled too. "You mean John the Baptist?"

"Yes. A gruesome story it is, yet I must say I am glad Herod has done the dirty work for us. It seems Herod held a great feast on his birthday, and while he and his princes were making merry, the daughter of Herodias danced before him. Herod was so pleased by her performance that he swore he would give her anything she asked for. And Salome—well-schooled by her mother, no doubt—went and asked Herodias." Shem shuddered. "Lord, save us from that cold-blooded woman. She instructed her daughter to ask for the head of John the Baptist on a platter!"

Eli recoiled in horror.

"They say Herod greatly repented of his oath,"

Shem went on. "But he was bound by his word. I hope Herodias is happy now."

Father gestured impatiently. "Whether or not Herodias is happy is none of our concern. John is dead, and it is my opinion that God can use even a wicked tetrarch to carry out His purposes."

Eli was aghast at such reasoning, but he dared say nothing. To his astonishment, Mother spoke up.

"Was God's purpose being carried out thirty years ago when Herod's father had all those babies killed in Bethlehem?" she asked.

"No need to dig up old stories from the past," Father snarled.

Later, when Father was asleep, Eli asked Mother, "What were you talking about? What babies were killed by Herod the Great?"

"Oh, there were rumors of a king being born in Bethlehem, and Herod was so frightened that he ordered all the babies two years old and under to be put to death."

"A king? Born in Bethlehem?" Eli exclaimed. "That's where the Scriptures say the Messiah is to come from!"

Mother shook her head. "Nothing much ever came of the rumors. Besides, if a king really had been born, he would hardly have escaped the murderous Herod."

But Eli was not convinced. "Couldn't God save His Messiah from a tetrarch?" He paused, thinking. "They say Jesus is a little over thirty years old . . ."

"But He's from Nazareth, in Galilee," Mother reminded him.

"That's right," agreed Eli, again confused.

Later, he lay awake on his goatskin, struggling with

questions. Jesus had called John His messenger. Why, then, had Jesus not saved him from the cruel Herodias? How could He let John become a victim of wanton lust? If Jesus were going to do great things, what was He waiting for?

ONE GLANCE at Asa's face next morning told Eli that Asa had already heard the awful news. "You must have heard the news," he murmured.

Asa's eyes were filled with pain. "Yes. Can you imagine the cruelty of those women?"

Eli thought of Sharon, who was probably about the same age as Herodias' daughter Salome. He shuddered. There was simply no comparing the purity and gentleness of the one and the wickedness of the other.

"But do you know," Asa went on, his voice brightening, "last night as I lay awake thinking about these things, it came to me that maybe there is still hope for John."

Eli stared at him, his basket of grapes forgotten. "Hope? But he is dead!"

"Yes. But we heard that Jesus once raised a man from the dead. He met a funeral procession near Nain one day, where a widow's only son was being carried out for burial." Asa paused, watching Eli's face. "We were told that when Jesus bade the young man arise, he sat up upon the bier."

"But you don't know whether it's true!" Eli exploded. "People do imagine things."

"Still . . . if it's true, Jesus might yet save John."

"He's buried already! Surely Jesus couldn't raise somebody from the grave," Eli objected.

Asa shrugged. "But if Jesus is really the Son of God, anything is possible," he said.

Eli began picking grapes rapidly. "A person would never guess that you are the son of a Sadducee, the way you talk about resurrection."

Asa looked pained. "That's beside the point. Listen, Eli... Maybe I'd better be quiet. You are not ready to listen. But will you listen if I talk about something else entirely?"

"Maybe," said Eli grudgingly.

"My father suggested we plan an outing for some of the young people who work here. He suggested a trip to the Jordan. That was before John was killed. At first when we heard the news, he thought we had better drop it. But then he realized a trip to the river could be a journey of remembrance."

"It's been a long time since I was last at the river," Eli said slowly. "When were you thinking of going?"

"Next week, possibly. The olive crop isn't good this year, so there will be a lull in farming just before the New Year. We would walk down one day—it's only about ten miles from here—and stay in Jericho for the night, then come back home the next day."

"Would the girls go too?" Eli asked.

Asa smiled. "Of course. Besides my sisters and Hannah and Joseph, we'd ask a few of the other workers as well."

"Sounds like an interesting trip," Eli said. "Father is reasonably well these days, so I should be able to leave him and Mother alone for one night."

A WEEK LATER Eli joined the merry group of young people setting out down the steep, winding road toward Jericho. In the ten miles of their journey they would descend some 3,800 feet, far below sea level.

"The air gets hotter and stuffier the farther down we get," Joseph remarked.

"The Jordan Valley is quite a change from the Judean hills," Eli agreed absently. His eyes were on Asa walking with his betrothed, Joseph's sister Hannah.

At last, when everybody was weary of the rocky, desert landscape, the Oasis of Jericho came into view. Jericho was a stately town, all green with date palms and orange groves. The group skirted Jericho and headed straight for the banks of the Jordan. The placid waters glowed in the light of the evening sun.

While the girls laid out a picnic meal, Asa remarked, "It's hard to imagine all the rapids and waterfalls in the upper regions of the Jordan when you see how calm the river is here."

Eli nodded. "I can't help thinking of John the Baptist when I'm here."

"I never came down to hear him," Asa said thoughtfully. "But Father told me how John's voice used to ring across the river as he called people to repentance."

"Next week, after the New Year, begin the Ten Days of Penitence that lead to the Day of Atonement," Eli said thoughtfully. "John's sermons on repentance would have been fitting for this time."

"You should have heard what Father said about the Ten Days of Penitence last night," Asa responded. "He says ten days are not enough. We ought to be repentant all the time! John and Jesus both said, 'Repent, for the kingdom of heaven is at hand!' Father says repentance is the requirement for entering the kingdom."

Questions sprang to Eli's mind, but just then the girls called that supper was ready. After the meal it was time to go to their lodging. Just outside Jericho was an inn where they planned to stay for the night. It was a crude little place, with the first story serving as a stable. Asa climbed the limestone steps, saying, "Girls, wait here while I go in to arrange your lodging with the keeper."

He returned shortly, his face unsmiling. "There's only one room available. Will that be enough?"

The girls looked at one another. "It will have to do," Sharon declared. "We don't want to sleep in the stable."

Asa grinned at the young men. "I guess that's what's left for us."

He led the way into the gloomy, dark-smelling lower portion. A cow lowed; several donkeys stamped impatient hooves. Asa whispered to Eli, "Here's a good place, in this empty stall." The two of them lay on the rustling straw, while the rest found spots at the other side of the stable.

"This must seem like poor lodging to you," Eli remarked, thinking of the fine curtains and rugs in the House Ben Simeon.

Asa chuckled. "Can't you just forget that I'm the son of a rich Sadducee? A stable should be good enough for me if it was good enough for Jesus to be born in."

"Jesus was born in a stable?" Eli repeated curiously.

"Didn't you know? Joseph of Nazareth and his betrothed wife, Mary, had to go to Bethlehem to be taxed. The little town was filled with people, and all the inns were occupied. So this couple resorted to the stable. And that night Jesus was born."

"So He *was* born in Bethlehem!" exclaimed Eli.

"Yes. Why is that so exciting?"

"Why, the prophets foretold that the Messiah would be born in Bethlehem. All this time I was puzzled about Jesus, because He's from Nazareth, in Galilee," explained Eli.

"I never studied the prophets very much, probably because Father is a Sadducee," Asa responded. "But he seems to be becoming less of a Sadducee. He now believes in the resurrection of the dead. And he's growing disillusioned about our customs; he speaks of disregarding the Day of Atonement."

"Hmmm," mused Eli. "And yet the 10th of Tishri is considered the most important in the Jewish calendar, because it provides atonement for all our sins."

Asa's voice came through the darkness. "Sometimes I wonder why we have to keep a special day for that. Don't the priests offer for sin every day?"

"It seems our sins require endless sacrifices," agreed Eli. "As though God is never truly satisfied with our repentance."

The straw crackled as Asa sought a more comfortable position. "Father keeps saying he expects something to happen that will end all these sacrifices someday."

"You mean, he expects something better to take their place?"

"That's right. He's not sure how it will happen, except that He's convinced it will have something to do with Jesus."

Chapter 13

"From what I hear, Jesus has been a real trial to the Pharisees," Simeon remarked one Sabbath to the usual group gathered at his house. His eyes twinkled at Eli. "Once he quoted some Scripture to a group of Pharisees, then challenged them to go and learn what the words meant."

"Imagine a man who has never gone to rabbinical school, telling Pharisees to study the Scriptures," chuckled Asa.

"What Scripture was it?" Eli wondered.

"Something from Hosea," Simeon replied. "Having been raised a Sadducee, I'm not very familiar with the prophets, but it went something like this: 'I desire mercy, and not sacrifice.'"

"Hmm," Eli said thoughtfully, "the rest of that passage goes like this: '. . . and the knowledge of God more than burned offerings.'"

"That reminds me of something else Jesus said," Simeon recalled. "He was speaking of the new kingdom, and He likened it to new wine, which we dare not put into old wineskins, lest they burst. New wine needs new wineskins."

"Meaning that His new kingdom cannot exist within our old system? Is that it?" questioned Isaiah.

Simeon nodded. "That's the way I understood it. Jesus is going to introduce something better than all these bloody sacrifices. Today is the Feast of Trumpets, and it makes my head swim to think of all the animals being slaughtered at the temple today."

"That passage in Hosea talks about sin and blood," Eli exclaimed. "'But they like men have transgressed the covenant: there have they dealt treacherously against me. Gilead is a city of them that work iniquity, and is polluted with blood . . .'"

The room was quiet as everyone absorbed the significance of these words. "Maybe it's Jerusalem—instead of Gilead—that should be called 'a city of them that work iniquity, and polluted with blood,'" Isaiah said soberly.

"The Master's teachings are such a contrast to the old Law. One day He proclaimed what life will be like in His kingdom, and His words were so beautiful . . ." Simeon consulted a letter in front of him. "'Blessed are the poor in spirit, for theirs is the kingdom of heaven. Blessed are those who mourn, for they shall be comforted. Blessed are the meek, for they shall inherit the earth. Blessed are those who hunger and thirst after righteousness, for they shall be satisfied . . .'" He looked up. "Imagine a kingdom full of peace and joy and righteousness!"

Hands clasped, eyes shining, Sharon exclaimed, "All those blessings are like a stream flowing from God!

84

Didn't Jesus say something to that Samaritan woman about a well of living water?"

Simeon looked pleased that she remembered. " 'Jesus said the water that He would give a person would be a well of water springing up into everlasting life.' "

Because of Eli's years with the rabbis, he remembered another passage from the Prophet Jeremiah that also spoke of living water. He quoted, " 'For my people have committed two evils; they have forsaken me the fountain of living waters, and hewed them out cisterns, broken cisterns, that can hold no water' " (Jeremiah 2:13).

"How meaningful those words are!" exclaimed Simeon. "When God first gave the old covenant, I believe it was like a living fountain of His Word. But Israel has forsaken the true spirit of God's Law and added hundreds of ordinances—and thus she has turned from the living fountain to broken cisterns."

"A poor trade, if you ask me," Asa commented dryly.

"You know," Simeon continued thoughtfully, "the Jordan River is a picture of Israel's falling away from the truth. At its source, the river is a stream of pure water gushing from the slopes of Mount Hermon. But look where it ends up—in the Dead Sea, a lake so far below sea level that it is nothing but a smelly, stagnant, and lifeless puddle."

"Not a very flattering picture," Isaiah commented.

Simeon smiled. "No wonder Jesus said, 'Unless your righteousness surpass that of the scribes and Pharisees, you shall not enter the kingdom of heaven.' You see, the laws of the new covenant go further than the old. Jesus says it is just as wrong to be angry with your brother as it is to murder him. Instead of saying 'an eye for an eye,' Jesus tells us not to resist evil."

Eli drew a long breath. "The laws of the new kingdom will be even harder to live up to than the old!"

Simeon nodded. "In fact, Jesus bids us to be perfect, even as God is perfect."

"How are we supposed to do that?" Eli asked with a hopeless gesture.

"I don't know," Simeon admitted. "But just wait— great things are in store. Jesus would not present these charges without some plan for carrying them out."

Chapter 14

"Tell me what they do at the Temple on this day," Isaac begged. It was the 10th of Tishri, the Day of Atonement, and Eli had gone over in the afternoon to visit the House Ben Isaiah. He and the two boys were relaxing upon the rooftop.

"Well, the first thing you might notice is that the High Priest does not wear his usual colorful, jeweled robe. On the Day of Atonement he wears pure white," Eli began.

Joseph nodded. "White is for purity. The high priest has to be pure himself if he's to offer an offering for all the people's sins."

"Yet strangely," Eli pointed out, "the high priest has to first make a sin offering for himself, because he's not without sin himself. That's the first thing they do after the regular morning sacrifices: a bullock is slain as a sin offering for the high priest. Then comes the moment that must surely be the high point of the high priest's year . . ."

"Is that when he goes into the holy of holies?" Isaac broke in excitedly.

Eli nodded. "He takes a censer of burning coals

and a vase of incense, and goes in through the vail that separates the holy of holies from the rest of the temple."

"Right into the presence of God!" marveled Joseph.

"What does he do in there?" Isaac wanted to know.

"He casts the incense upon the burning coals to create a cloud of smoke that will 'cover the mercy seat.'"

"Exactly what God told Moses to do many years ago," Joseph put in.

"Then the high priest returns to get some of the bullock's blood," Eli went on. "This he takes back within the vail to sprinkle onto the mercy seat, and also seven times upon the ground before it. When he comes back out, it is time to slay the goat for the sin offering."

"But aren't there two goats?" Joseph questioned.

"Yes, but only one is slain in the temple. Then the high priest makes his third trip within the vail, this time with the blood of the goat, to make atonement for all the people. Some of that blood is also mixed with the blood of the bullock and sprinkled in certain places near the altar, to make atonement for the temple, the court, the altar, and all the furniture."

"It goes around in circles, doesn't it?" Isaac observed thoughtfully. "They even have to make atonement for the things they use to make atonement!"

Eli smiled. "I guess you're right." In his mind he pictured the Dead Sea, turned bright red by the blood of all the offerings.

"Isn't it time for the second goat next?" Joseph prompted.

"Yes. Now the high priest lays his hands on the other goat and quotes words from the Torah, 'And Aaron shall lay both his hands upon the head of the live goat, and confess over him all the iniquities of the children of Israel, and all their transgressions in all their sins, putting them upon the head of the goat.' " He looked at Isaac. "Don't you think that's an ugly burden to bear? All the sins of Israel?"

The boy nodded soberly. "And the goat has to die because of that burden, doesn't he?"

"Yes. They take him into the wilderness and shove him off a high cliff—though the poor goat never committed a sin himself," Joseph said.

"That's the whole idea behind the offerings, I guess," Eli mused. "A sinless victim for the sinner."

The picture of that hapless goat was still vivid in Eli's mind the next day. "Asa," he said, "I can't forget that goat we talked about."

"You know what John the Baptist said at the Jordan months ago when Jesus passed by? 'Behold the Lamb of God, who takes away the sin of the world!' "

Eli stared. "Lamb of God?"

Asa nodded. "And just this past week Father was reading the prophets, and he came upon a passage which he felt certain is connected with John's words, something about everybody having gone astray like sheep, and a lamb being brought to the slaughter..."

"Oh, that's from Isaiah," Eli interrupted. " 'All we like sheep have gone astray; we have turned every one to his own way; and the Lord hath laid on him the iniquity of us all. He was oppressed, and he was afflicted, yet he opened not his mouth: he is brought as a lamb to the slaughter, and as a sheep before her shearers is dumb, so he openeth not his mouth.' "

"That's it," agreed Asa. "Father thinks those words refer to the Messiah—to Jesus."

Eli glanced at the two yoke of oxen, patiently switching their tails while their young plowman chatted. Then he lifted his eyes to the hills beyond the village. " 'The Lord has laid on him the iniquity of us all,' " he mused. "Is your father saying that the sins of the people will be laid on Jesus, like that poor scapegoat in the temple? But how could that be?"

"Well," Asa said slowly, "Father has heard that Jesus sometimes speaks as though He expects to die before long. Once He referred to the Prophet Jonah." He looked guiltily at the waiting oxen, then hurried on, "I'll tell the story as quickly as I can. The Pharisees had been giving Jesus a hard time, and Jesus was quite sharp with them, calling them a generation of vipers . . ."

"Jesus called the Pharisees that?" Eli interrupted with astonishment.

"So I heard," Asa agreed. "They were offended, of course, and demanded that Jesus show them a sign to prove He has the authority to do and say such things. Then Jesus replied, 'No sign will be given this generation except the sign of the Prophet Jonah. As Jonah was in the belly of the whale for three days and three nights, so shall the Son of Man be in the heart of the earth for three days and three nights.' "

Eli knit his brows. "In the heart of the earth? Was He saying He's going to die and be buried?"

"Father thinks so. It's a mystery to me."

"But how could Jesus be a Deliverer and set up a

kingdom if He died?" Eli protested.

Asa shook his head. "I don't know. But think of the temple sacrifices. Some creature always has to die to atone for the people's sins."

Eli stared at his friend. "You mean—Jesus would somehow be made a sacrifice, like those goats and rams and bullocks slaughtered by the priests? But how . . . ?" His voice trailed off. Through his mind floated a gruesome vision of the Pharisees binding Jesus and laying Him upon the Altar of Sacrifice. He shuddered. "Surely not!"

Asa shrugged and turned toward the oxen.

Eli called after him, "Why do you think Jesus put a time limit on His stay in the heart of the earth? Wouldn't He remain in the grave if He died?"

Asa looked back. "I asked my father that question. All he said was Jesus has proven He can raise the dead to life."

Eli shook his head slowly. Then he spoke to his oxen, which leaned into the traces while the plowshare struggled with the grudging soil.

Chapter 15

"We are going to have a booth for the Feast of Tabernacles this year," Father decided on the 14th of Tishri. "'Ye shall dwell in booths seven days; all that are Israelites born shall dwell in booths,'" Father quoted from the Law.

"But invalids are exempt from dwelling in booths," Mother objected.

Father pointed a bony finger at Eli. "My son is not an invalid! And he *is* an Israelite born." He paused for breath. "Besides, I am better than I was last year and able to dwell in a booth."

"You mean we would have to carry you to the house-top?" Mother asked in consternation.

Father shook his head. "The booth need not be on the housetop. The courtyard will do."

"But the courtyard is so small . . . and I need the space for cooking and grinding," Mother protested.

"Silence, woman! You can have our house to your-self and your cooking while Eli and I live in the court-yard!" Father's voice was shrill with irritation.

"Yes, yes. That will do," Mother said meekly.

Father turned to Eli. "Find someone to help build our booth. That boy of Isaiah's would do. And don't forget the *etrog,* and the branches for the *lulab!*"

"Yes, Father." Eli felt overwhelmed by all he was expected to accomplish today. He hurried to the House Ben Isaiah to ask for help. Isaac, whose father was not going to build a booth, quickly joined him, eager to help.

"Are there any vendors selling branches in this village?" Eli asked him. "We don't have time to go out and cut any."

"Yes, down by the goat shed." Isaac tugged at his hand. "Did you see those pilgrims passing through here yesterday on their way to Jerusalem? The city must be full of booths if all the pilgrims need them."

"The strangers will share the local people's booths," Eli pointed out.

"Did Asa go up to Jerusalem for the feast?" Isaac asked.

Eli nodded.

"I guess he hopes to see Jesus there," Isaac said shrewdly.

Eli looked down at his little friend. "Maybe so." How he wished he were in the city with Asa this week, instead of being stuck here building a booth for a father who would probably be very hard to please.

He was right. Father asked him to carry his pallet to the courtyard where he could keep a sharp eye on the erection of the flimsy shelter. It had to have at least three sides. And, though the branches were to be thatched loosely enough to permit a view of the stars at night, the structure was to provide more shade than sun. Eli toiled dutifully, changing a branch here or adding another there, under his father's critical instructions.

It was almost sundown when Father said grudgingly, "I guess it will have to do. You still haven't brought the branches for the *lulab*."

Eli and Isaac set out once more for the goat shed. "I know the words of the Law about the *lulab* and the *etrog*," Isaac said importantly. " 'And ye shall take you on the first day the fruit of goodly trees, branches of palm trees, and the boughs of thick trees, and willows of the brook; and ye shall rejoice before the Lord your God seven days.' "

The Pharisees took these words to mean that every Israelite was to carry in his right hand a bouquet, or *lulab*, consisting of a palm, a willow, and a myrtle branch; and in his left hand was to be the *etrog*—a citron to signify the "fruit of goodly trees."

"I wish I could sleep in your booth tonight," Isaac said when they returned to the House Ben Amos.

"Did you ask your father whether you may stay?" asked Mother, bringing out a pot of stew and setting it down in the booth. All their meals would be eaten there during the festive week.

"No, I didn't ask, so I must go home," Isaac admitted reluctantly. He watched Mother preparing the meal under the leafy shelter. "Everything is turned around for her. Usually she cooks outdoors in the summer and carries food indoors to eat."

Eli smiled. "Now before you go home will you please help me move Father's pallet into the booth?"

Father smiled at the youngster with rare good

humor. "Why don't you invite your parents to eat the festive meal with us tomorrow?"

Eli was so astonished that he nearly dropped his end of the pallet. What had come over Father?

"Oh, I'm sure they'll come," Isaac promised happily. He hurried home, gleefully waving his *lulab*.

The next day after the meal, the three boys chose to walk down to the grove. "In Jerusalem I would have watched the ceremony of the drawing of water this morning," Eli mused, well aware that this would bring a torrent of questions from Isaac.

He was not disappointed. The youngster begged him to tell about the ceremony, so he sat down with his back against a tree trunk and began. "Everybody wants to watch the procession coming down to the Pool of Siloam from the temple. At the head is a priest carrying a golden pitcher, and after him come hundreds of people, singing and waving their *lulabs.*"

"They must look like a walking forest, with all those branches," Isaac observed.

"Exactly," agreed Eli. "The priest comes to the pool and draws water into his pitcher, and then they all parade back to the temple. There, the great altar has been decorated with willow branches, and all the people watch while the priests pour water and wine into the basins."

"Is that when everybody starts shouting, 'Raise thy hand'?" Joseph asked.

Eli nodded.

"Why do they do that?" Isaac wondered.

"Well, it's a long story," Eli told him. When Isaac assured him that he liked long stories, Eli began. "The whole thing has to do with the disagreements between the Pharisees and the Sadducees. I guess you know there are lots of things they don't agree on. One of them is how to carry out this ceremony. Some 120 years ago, Jannaeus, a Sadducean high priest, poured the water onto the ground instead of into the basins, just to show his contempt for the Pharisees. They were so angry that they began pelting him with their *etrogs*!"

"Really!" marveled Isaac. "I thought you have to hang on to your *etrog* for a whole week."

"When people are angry enough, they do strange things," Eli answered. "What happened next was tragic. Soldiers were called out because of the ruckus, and 6,000 people were slain."

Isaac gave a low whistle. "Six thousand! That must have been horrible."

"And ever since that," Eli concluded, "the people call out, 'Raise thy hand!' to make sure the priest has really poured the water into the basin and not onto the ground."

"I see," said Isaac. "And how many sacrifices are there on this day?"

"Festive ones? Thirteen bullocks, two rams, fourteen lambs, and one goat. Right, Joseph?"

The other nodded. "I think so. And that's the same every day this week, except that each day there'll be one less bullock. Twelve tomorrow, eleven the next day, and so on, until the seventh day there are only seven."

Joseph got to his feet. "It's getting toward sundown. I'd better go home and milk those goats."

Eli chose to stay in the grove a while longer,

watching the sun set beyond the Judean hills. As his mind replayed the water-drawing ceremony at Siloam, he recalled those words from Jeremiah about "broken cisterns." What were these old customs, anyway, except "broken cisterns" that caused strife and unrest? Could they compare at all with the fresh, new streams of living water Jesus had promised, with their blessings of peace and joy and righteousness?

Chapter 16

A cold rain slashed at Eli as he walked home after another Sabbath meal at the House Ben Simeon. He hardly noticed the dampness seeping through his cloak as he brooded on the things he had heard. Today, it seemed to him, he had been given an ultimatum: Make up your mind! Either you follow Jesus, or you don't!

It began when Simeon told how the Pharisees kept hounding Jesus, watching His every step, and accusing Him of breaking the Sabbath. Simeon's wife, Lana, had said that Jesus was in real danger.

But Simeon had disagreed. "I believe it's the Pharisees who are in danger. Once Jesus told a parable of a man who sowed good seed in his field, but the wicked one came along and sowed tares as well. At the harvest, the workers burned the tares while the wheat was gathered into the barn."

"Tell us the meaning of the parable," Sharon had requested.

"I believe Jesus Himself is the sower of the good seed, sown on the whole earth like a field..." Simeon said.

"The whole earth?" Asa had interrupted. "But Jesus stays mostly in one small part of the earth, Galilee!"

"His Word is the seed," Simeon had explained. "Like a stream of living water, His Word cannot stay in one little spot. It is destined to flow through all the world!"

Eli had found this vision mind-boggling. But Simeon had gone on to challenge his family. "Who are we? Are we those who accept the good seed, and grow to harvest? Or are we like the Pharisees, tares reserved for the fires of hell?"

Now those words were ringing in Eli's ears. What did it really mean for him? Did it mean disobeying his father, who seemed to identify himself with the tares in the Master's parable? Did it mean he should go up to Galilee and find Jesus?

Before he would do that, there was one thing he needed to find out. Eli made up his mind to ask his Mother about it this very night. But when he arrived at home, Father was awake and impatient to be served his evening meal. While he ate, Father fixed his faded eyes on Eli. "You were at the Sadducee's house again." His voice held an ominous note.

"Yes," quavered Eli. He waited tensely, fearing what he would hear next.

But Father remained silent, fumbling the bread to his mouth with withered hands.

Much later, after Father had gone to sleep, Eli joined Mother on the housetop. Quickly, before his courage left him, he began, "What do you think Father would say if I requested his permission to ask for Sharon's hand in marriage?"

He wished the night were not so dark, so that he could see her face and know whether this was a complete surprise for her. From her voice he could only guess.

"Well! The daughter of a rich man," she said.

"I know. I can hardly believe that it would be possible, but Asa assures me his father would be pleased if I asked. The only reason I have not is because of . . . of Father."

Mother was silent for a long time. "I guess you will just have to ask Father and see. I doubt that Father knows about Simeon's interest in the teachings of Jesus. As long as he doesn't know that, you may have a chance."

"And you, Mother. Do you mind that I would ask the daughter of Simeon?" It was important to know how she felt.

"Not at all," she said without hesitation. "I was expecting this, Eli."

"Oh!" exclaimed Eli. "But I never said anything about Sharon, did I?"

"No. But I am not blind."

"But Father—he doesn't suspect, does he? Will it be a complete surprise for him?"

"I think so. But, as I said, you have to ask and see."

After morning prayers the next day, Eli approached his father. Trying to keep his voice steady, he said, "Father, I am thinking of asking Simeon for the hand of his daughter."

"Simeon!" The words left Father's lips like an explosion. Food splattered from his mouth onto the table. "Simeon is a follower of that blasphemer!"

Consternation flooded Mother's face. "But he is dead," she said quickly. "John is now dead."

"Silence, woman! I don't mean John. Simeon is a follower of Jesus!"

"How did you know?" Eli asked without thinking.

"You thought you could pull this off behind your sick father's back? My body may be sick, but my mind is not. I can still understand the things that are told to me." Father paused to regain his breath. "You have your answer. I can never approve of your asking Sharon. I have been debating whether I should forbid you to go to the House Ben Simeon. Now I know what to say. You must stay away from that home! He will fill you with blasphemy, that Sadducee!"

Eli moved blindly to the courtyard. Mother followed, wordlessly handing him his scrip. The pain in her eyes spoke more than words.

For the first time since their friendship began, Eli dreaded meeting Asa. He managed to avoid running into him during the forenoon, but when Asa beckoned to him from a secluded spot where he intended to eat lunch, Eli knew he could no longer put off his unpleasant task.

After he had eaten in silence for some minutes, Asa asked gently, "Do you have something on your mind?"

Eli nodded miserably. "Father has forbidden me to enter your home."

"Oh!" his friend exclaimed in shock. "Is it . . . did you say something about Sharon to him?"

"Yes. Mother thought Father might not know about your father being a follower of Jesus. But he knew. Uncle Shem must have told him." Eli looked up. "I feel so . . . humiliated."

Asa seemed at a loss for words. Like Eli, he had lost interest in his food and was staring out over the valley.

Eli went on desperately, "Why don't I just leave home? I long to be near Jesus anyway. I could go up to Capernaum."

Eli leaned forward. "Tell me, Asa. Is there any possibility that Sharon would consent to go away with me? Would your father let her?"

Asa drew back, his face troubled. "Aren't you taking things too far? Think it over before you make such reckless decisions."

"Then help me make my decision," Eli urged. "Find out what your father thinks. Find out what Sharon thinks. Can you?"

Asa was silent for another long moment. Then he said reluctantly, "Yes, I will find out. Because you are my friend." He rose to his feet. "For now we had better get back to work."

Having shared his desperate plan with someone, Eli's heart felt lighter. He resolved to accept Simeon's guidance, regardless of what it would be.

Eagerly he took the letter Asa gave him the next morning, and slipped behind a boulder to read it. "Be patient, Eli," Simeon had written. "Wait. I believe great things are in store for Jesus. One day He will break the bounds of time and geography and become available to everyone, all the time, all at once. Someday this living stream of God's Word will water all the land! I don't know how Jesus will do it, but He will have a way.

"Concerning Sharon, there too, I say, wait. I talked

with her and she agrees. She will wait for you. I believe a way will be opened for the two of you, but you will have to wait.

"Eli, your life just now may seem like a boat tossing on a stormy sea. Did you know that Jesus was once in a boat on the Sea of Galilee with His disciples when a storm arose? You know what those storms are like: the winds rush down from the surrounding hills to stir the water like a great wooden spoon stirring a brew. His disciples were very frightened; they found Jesus asleep in the bow of the ship.

" 'Master, save us! We perish!' they cried. Jesus awoke and said, 'Why are you so fearful, you of little faith?' Then He stood and rebuked the winds and the sea: 'Peace, be still.' Immediately there was a great calm.

"You see, Eli, we believe Jesus will yet do great things, if even the wind obeys Him. We must have faith in Him."

Tears flowed freely down Eli's cheeks. There behind the boulder he did something he had rarely done before. He lifted his heart in spontaneous prayer to God. "Show me Your way, Lord. Help me to work patiently until I, too, may see Jesus."

Truly, it was like a great calm after a storm at sea.

Chapter 17

Asa and Hannah were getting married. Eli tried very hard to be glad for his friend and forget about his own disappointments. As he walked home with Joseph one evening, Joseph talked excitedly about his sister's wedding.

"The House Ben Simeon will supply wedding garments for the friends of the groom. Have you heard that?"

Eli nodded. "Yes, I have," he said hesitantly. "But I don't know whether I'll be at the wedding."

"Why not?" demanded Joseph in amazement.

"I thought you knew. Father has forbidden me to go to the House Ben Simeon."

"I see. Because he is a follower of Jesus?" When Eli nodded, Joseph said, "Well, I think your father has good sense."

Eli stared at his sandaled feet. What a mixed-up world this was! But then, hadn't Jesus said His teachings would bring strife to families?

"Sometimes I wish Father had forbidden Hannah to marry Asa. They're heading for trouble, if you ask me," Joseph said gloomily.

Eli could not think what to say. He was glad he had reached home, and could bid his neighbor *shalom* for now.

Mother was cheerful when she saw him. "You are home early!" she said.

He glanced at her questioningly and saw a hint of suppressed excitement in her face. She put her finger to her lips and cautioned, "Yes, I have something to tell you. But not now."

It was cold upon the housetop at this time of year, but that was where Eli and Mother went after Father was snoring. The village had a ghostly appearance by moonlight. On the faraway hills was a gleam of snow.

Mother drew her cloak more closely about her. "You may go to the wedding! I reasoned with Father, and he agreed."

"He did?" exclaimed Eli.

"And I will be able to watch the bridal procession right here from our housetop. Only a few more weeks now!" Mother went on happily.

The first pink blooms had appeared in the almond trees by the time of the wedding, which was in the month of Shebat. Twilight was falling when the first strains of music told Eli the bridal procession was starting off. He and Mother hurried to the housetop, where they could easily see the House Ben Isaiah.

First came the musicians and dancers, followed by those who bore the bride's household goods and linens. Then came the bride, also walking, but covered by a colorful canopy held over her by the bridal party. Somewhere among them, Eli knew, was Sharon. What a splendid sight the procession made, lighted by many flaring torches held aloft! They watched until the procession wound out of sight, up the hill toward the House Ben Simeon.

"Hadn't you better leave now?" urged Mother.

"Yes, I suppose so." Clad in the wedding garment provided by Asa, Eli hurried away. The bridegroom's party was to meet at the home of Asa's uncle, Adam, where Asa himself was now waiting. When word came that the bride had reached his father's house, the bridegroom would set out with his procession.

The torches were already lit when Eli arrived, and people were milling about Adam's courtyard. There in the midst was Asa, appearing slightly dazed. His face lit up at the sight of Eli. "I thought you would never come!"

"I watched the bridal procession first," Eli explained breathlessly.

"Was it nice?" Asa asked eagerly.

"Oh, yes. Hannah is waiting for you now."

Suddenly a shout arose, off to one side of the courtyard.

"What is that smell?" Asa asked in alarm.

Eli wrinkled his nose. "Something's burning!"

A man pushed his way breathlessly to the bridegroom. "Do you have an extra wedding garment? Haman Bar Benjamin was careless with his torch and burned his robe."

"What of the boy? Is he all right?" inquired Asa.

"He says so. Someone has given him ointment for his burns. He insists he wants to be included in the procession," replied the other.

"An extra robe," reflected Asa. "No, I have none.

But here—he can have mine." With that, he drew off his own white robe and handed it to the astounded man. "I was too warm anyway. It's time we left. They will wonder what has happened to our procession," Asa insisted.

Shaking his head in astonishment, the man bore away the robe. Eli was deeply touched by his friend's generous gesture.

At last they were off, and none too soon, for midnight was approaching. "Do you think the bridesmaids' lamps had enough oil to stay lighted all this time?" Eli asked. The friends of the bride, including Sharon, were to carry lighted lamps and meet the bridegroom's procession.

"Depends on whether they thought to bring extra oil," Asa answered. "I know Sharon planned to take an extra vessel."

Late though it was, many people were still awake, watching the procession. From housetop after housetop rang the glad shout, "Behold, the bridegroom comes! He comes!"

Soon the winking lights of the bridesmaids' lamps came into view. But off to one side, Eli noticed several girls slinking away, carrying unlit lamps. Maybe they were out of oil and hoping to refill their lamps in time to be back at the House Ben Simeon to enter before the doors closed behind the bridegroom's procession.

The procession swept through the entrance and across the courtyard, advancing to the inner room where the bride waited beneath a brilliant canopy. Just before the bridegroom reached the canopy, an insistent thumping was heard at the outer door. "It's the bridesmaids who went for more oil," someone whispered. "They came back too late. The door will not be opened for them again."

For a moment Eli pitied the poor girls who had not brought enough oil. Then he spied Sharon standing near the canopy, and he quickly forgot the others. His heart throbbed with joy for Asa as he took his place beneath the canopy.

Strangely, Eli thought of John the Baptist as the rabbi performed the marriage rites. Had not John called himself a mere "friend of the Bridegroom" as Jesus' fame overwhelmed his own? Had he not expressed joy that he could hear the Bridegroom's voice?

Because of the ache in his heart when he looked at Sharon, Eli thought he knew how John must have felt. Had he gone on rejoicing even when he was shut up in that lonely prison? Had he faced a gruesome death with peace in his heart, knowing the true Bridegroom had come?

But if Jesus were the Bridegroom, who was the bride? For Eli, it was a question without an answer.

Chapter 18

Passover came and went. Neither Simeon nor Asa went up to Jerusalem for the Feast, but as far as they could tell, Jesus had not been there either. For Eli this knowledge was another dark cloud in an already-dark sky. If Jesus really was who Simeon hoped, then why didn't He come? Surely Jerusalem would be a better place to set up a kingdom than some out-of-the-way village in Galilee!

Uncle Shem had been up for the Feast, though. One evening he came gloating to the House Ben Amos with news of Jesus. Eli's heart sank as he listened to the conversation.

"Perhaps it is just as well that the Sanhedrin could never stop Jesus' activities," Shem began. "It's ending up the usual story of anyone who proclaims himself Messiah. The fame of Jesus is winding down now, and His followers are turning away."

"Oh?" said Father doubtfully. "Two years ago you told me Jesus had been discredited because He talked with an immoral Samaritan woman. Yet, since then, His fame has only grown."

Shem shrugged. "It only goes to show what poor judgment the rabble has. They are at last catching on to what we already saw two years ago. Jesus is untrustworthy, a blasphemer, and perhaps even insane."

"Hmm. What makes you say that?"

"Who but a man gone crazy would start insisting that people must eat of his flesh and drink of his blood if they want to live forever? I have it from reliable sources that Jesus is spouting such nonsense. He has lost most of his following because of it."

"Ah. The truth wins out in the end," Father said smugly. After a moment's thought, he asked, "But do you mean that the Sanhedrin thinks they can now sit back and relax? If Jesus is insane, isn't that all the more reason for taking Him into custody before He does something really dangerous? He is still a lawbreaker, inciting our people to forsake the holy Law. Did you not hear about the big outdoor feast Jesus held one day? Perhaps 'orgy' would be a better word for it. There were thousands of people—and they all ate with unwashed hands!"

"Unwashed hands!" exclaimed Shem, horrified. "So Jesus defies the laws of cleanliness?"

"You see what I mean," Father said self-righteously. "Why don't you do something about it, Shem? Persuade the Sanhedrin to send someone to Galilee and arrest this dangerous man!"

Shem shifted uncomfortably. "You must realize that I have not much influence with the Sanhedrin."

"Still, at least say something!" Father spat out. "It's high time something is done. Oh, if only I were well . . ."

"Yes, yes," Shem soothed, alarmed at Father's agitation. "I will do what I can. Tomorrow I am riding back to Jerusalem, and I will tell them what you recommended."

Father looked pleased as he bade his half brother *shalom*.

As for Eli, he climbed despondently to his bedchamber. His vision of Jesus as a King had been demolished. In its place was a humiliating picture of an insane man, mouthing crude nonsense to a fast-diminishing crowd. The long night watches passed sleeplessly. He longed to tell Asa what Shem had said. Surely Asa would have heard another, more positive side to this sordid tale!

Working beside Asa in the barley field the next day, Eli told him what Shem had said. Asa was troubled. "How strange this sounds! Do you think Shem really knows?"

Eli felled a clump of barley with a savage swing of his sickle. "I hope not! I thought perhaps you knew another version of the story."

"If Father knows anything about this feast, and the Master offering His flesh to eat, I have not heard him speak about it," Asa replied. "I will certainly ask him tonight! In fact, I could go up to the house for lunch and speak to him."

"Please do," Eli urged. "I can hardly wait to set my mind at rest."

Later when Asa returned to the fields, Eli gave him an eager, questioning glance. But Asa shook his head. "Father knows nothing about it. He admitted he was starting to wonder why he has not received any letters from Galilee recently. He has friends up there, you know, who used to keep him informed about the doings of Jesus."

"Used to," Eli repeated sadly. "Then perhaps Shem was right, and they have all deserted Jesus."

"Father does not give up his dreams so easily," Asa replied. "He is setting off for Jerusalem today, in hopes of getting to the root of the matter."

"That's good," said Eli, somewhat cheered. "But he can't stop Uncle Shem from inciting the Sanhedrin to take Jesus into custody. For all I know, a deputation has started north already."

Asa chuckled. "They'll be taking the river route, no doubt, so it'll be four or five days before they ever get to Capernaum."

"Still, they'll get there eventually, and it will be because my father advised them to go," Eli said miserably.

"Cheer up," Asa advised. "Father will be back from Jerusalem in a day or two. He may learn that Shem's stories were false, and even if they are true, Jesus is perfectly safe from a bunch of angry Pharisees. God won't let them touch Him."

Eli gazed at his friend, deeply impressed with his confidence. "I wish I had your faith."

Asa shrugged. "If you were around my father all the time, the way I am, you would have to have faith in the Master too." Though married now, Asa still lived in the House Ben Simeon with his wife.

SIMEON'S FAITH, as it turned out, was not misplaced. A few days later Asa had glowing stories to tell

114

of how Jesus had fed 5,000 people in the wilderness with only a few loaves and a few fishes; and how afterwards twelve baskets full of leftovers were gathered up. "So you see," Asa declared, "the Pharisees looked beyond a great miracle and saw only that the people had eaten with unwashed hands."

"You make me ashamed to be the son of a Pharisee," Eli confessed. "But what of that other story, about eating the Master's flesh and drinking His blood?"

"Well," said Asa, "the crowd nearly went crazy with adoration after the miracle of the loaves. They tried to make Jesus king. But He would have none of it—He simply slipped out of their hands and disappeared."

"Why?" came Eli's bewildered question. "He would have had enough men right there for an army!"

"I asked Father the same thing, and he almost laughed," Asa admitted. "He asked how I thought that would fit with the teachings of Jesus, to be made king upon the whim of an excited crowd with satisfied stomachs? Jesus calls us to repentance, Father said, and repentance comes before the kingdom. The crowd was not repentant. Father doesn't believe Israel is ready yet for the kingdom of Jesus."

"Sometimes I wonder when we ever will be ready," Eli muttered.

"When we begin to understand the spiritual meaning of the Master's words," Asa replied promptly. "Father learned that Jesus did tell the people He was the bread of life, which comes down from heaven. Jesus said people who come to Him, will not hunger or thirst. 'He who eats my flesh and drinks my blood has eternal life!' Jesus said."

Eli's heart sank. Through his mind floated a picture of temple priests, gorging themselves with meat sacrificed on the altar. "But what does Jesus mean by these strange words? I can understand why people might have turned away from Him."

Asa grasped his arm, hard. "Don't talk like that! Oh, I wish you could hear Father . . ." His voice trailed off. "I'm sorry. I shouldn't have said that, because I know you can't. But Father is quite thrilled by the spiritual beauty of these words. If only I could convey his feelings to you. Father told Mother that Israel is at last receiving manna from heaven again! How sad that we are too blind to realize it!"

"Manna from heaven," Eli repeated wonderingly.

"You see, Jesus tried to explain to the crowd that the flesh doesn't profit anything; that His words are spirit and life. Much like He said to the Samaritan woman that true worshipers have to serve God in spirit. Remember?"

"Yes," said Eli slowly. A new understanding was beginning to dawn.

"The crowd refused to see and understand. But my father is far from deserting Jesus, and you and I will listen to him. Right?" Asa concluded fervently, closing his scrip and getting to his feet.

"Right," agreed Eli with a smile.

Chapter 19

"I have news for you, Eli," Asa said one day during the wheat harvest.

Eli searched Asa's face, wondering what it could be. "Have you heard how things went for the deputation of Pharisees that visited Jesus in Galilee?" he asked.

Asa looked blank. "What? Oh, no. I'd almost forgotten about that. No, it's something about Hannah and me. We have bought a house!"

"You have! Here in Ashbaroth, I hope? I hadn't heard that any houses were for sale up on the hill."

"What makes you think we want to live in the rich part of town?" Asa asked, laughing. "Surely you heard that the home of Jerub the potter was for sale."

"You've bought Jerub's place? But that's on our street!" exclaimed Eli in disbelief.

"Well, why not? My wife is from your street, is she not?" Asa exclaimed. "Not only are we going to live there, but I plan to carry on Jerub's trade as well."

Eli shook his head slowly. "The son of a rich Sadducee—making clay pots."

Asa pretended to be offended. "Is pottery-making worse than working as a farmer?"

Only then did it dawn on Eli what this new turn of events would mean. "Then you won't be working in the fields with me any more!" he cried.

"No, but listen, Eli. You'll be able to visit me at our home, and what's more, you could meet my father there without going against your father's wishes," Asa pointed out.

"That's right," Eli agreed. "It will be good to see him again." *And Sharon,* his heart was saying. *I might meet Sharon there, too, sometime.*

"So are you moving soon?" Eli asked.

"In a week or two, when the wheat has all been cut. I am going to ask Father to let you off from work so that you can help me," Asa confided.

The thought put a bounce into Eli's step all day. At nightfall, however, his spirits sank when Uncle Shem appeared once more at their door. Would he have news of the deputation? Was Jesus in prison now? As Shem drew nearer to the lamp in Father's room, Eli noted that Shem's face wore no look of triumph.

Perhaps Father sensed this too, for he challenged Shem immediately. "Were they successful?" he snapped.

Shem took time to make himself comfortable upon the goatskin near Father's pallet. "Well, they found Jesus anyway."

Silence hung heavy in the room.

"But they haven't taken Him into custody?" Father rasped.

Shem shook his head.

"Why?" Father shouted.

"They . . . they claimed Jesus overwhelmed them," Shem said, gesturing.

"An unlettered Galilean, rumored to be insane, *overwhelmed* some members of the Sanhedrin? What are you talking about?" Father demanded angrily.

"Jesus accused them of setting aside the commandments of God in favor of men's traditions. And . . ."

"*He* accused them! But I thought *they* were doing the accusing!" Father snarled.

"That's what we asked the Pharisees when they returned. But they said, 'You weren't there. You don't know what it's like to confront that man. He stood there quoting Isaiah at us . . .' "

"Quoting Isaiah?"

"Yes. He called them hypocrites and said, 'Isaiah has well prophesied concerning you, saying, This people honors me with their lips, but their heart is far from Me; But in vain do they worship Me, teaching as doctrines the commandments of men.' "

"He said that about important members of the Sanhedrin?" Father's usually pale face darkened. "And they walked away without taking Him into custody?"

Shem shrugged as though weary of bearing the brunt of Father's wrath. "Don't blame me. Those who were there said they . . . they were rendered powerless just by the way Jesus looked at them."

"Rendered powerless?" Father's voice rose to a shriek.

Uncle Shem got to his feet. "That's what they said. Look, I wasn't happy to tell you about this, and you certainly didn't make it easy for me. Once more I remind you, I am not to blame for the Sanhedrin's incompetence," he said indignantly. Turning, he stalked from the House Ben Amos without so much as a parting shalom.

Eli marveled as he prepared for bed. In the room below, he could hear his father still muttering angrily. At times his voice rose to a shout. Poor Mother! She would have to listen until he calmed down.

The next morning Eli whispered to Mother as she put food into his scrip, "Today is Asa's moving day. Instead of going to the fields, I'll go down the street to the potter's house to help unload the beasts when Asa's things arrive."

Mother's wan face looked weary, but she smiled nevertheless. "You are glad Asa will be living nearby."

Eli nodded. "They even plan to attend our synagogue."

"Ah. Hannah will feel more at home here than she did at the synagogue on the hill," Mother commented.

"Was she unhappy?"

"Oh, I don't know. Her mother told me Hannah missed her friends down here."

Eli walked slowly to the potter's house, reflecting upon his friend's reasons for moving. Asa was already there with the first load of household goods. As Eli helped carry things inside he told him about Uncle Shem's visit.

"So there you have it," Asa chuckled when Eli had finished. "God takes care of His own!"

Eli nodded, ashamed. "I should not have been so fearful," he said.

Asa set down a bundle of bedding. "You remind me

of something that happened right after the crowd tried to make Jesus king, and He disappeared. Jesus' disciples ended up taking a ship across the sea to Capernaum, where they must have thought they might find Him.

"Anyway, during the night a storm arose on the sea. The disciples became quite frightened. Soon they saw something that frightened them even more, someone walking toward them on the waves! It was Jesus, and He called to them, 'It is I, be not afraid.'

"One of His disciples is Peter, an impulsive fellow. He actually got out of the ship with the intention of walking on the water too! He challenged Jesus, 'If it's really You, tell me to come to You.' And when Jesus answered, 'Come,' he set out."

"I would have been afraid," Eli admitted.

"So would I. And so was Peter! Pretty soon he started sinking, and howled to Jesus for rescue. Jesus grabbed his hand and asked, 'Why did you doubt? You have so little faith.' Apparently it wasn't until Peter started doubting that he began to sink. Father says it's just another indication that we have to believe in the Master's power if we want to see Him do great things."

Asa glanced toward the street behind Eli. "Here are the women now," he said.

Eli turned quickly. Walking toward him were Hannah and her four sisters-in-law, smiling brightly. It was the first time in months that Eli had seen Sharon, and he felt overwhelmed. She gave him a shy smile before entering the house.

Asa was watching him. "I hope we haven't brought too many things for this little house. Let's go in and help them arrange furniture."

"You could easily do that," Eli said with a wry smile as he followed him inside. Though he and Sharon never spoke to each other that day, he was happy simply to be around her again and to see her face.

Chapter 20

The summer passed happily for Eli. As often as he dared, he went to the House Ben Asa, sometimes to visit them and sometimes to meet the family of Simeon. Often the family of Isaiah was there too. When they were, there was always news of Jesus.

Eli heard how Jesus fed another group of 4,000 people with only a handful of food, this time on the east side of the sea near Decapolis. He heard how an evil spirit was cast out of a Canaanite woman's daughter, and how Jesus healed a deaf and dumb man.

Jesus seemed always to be in danger. "Even the Sadducees are on His trail now," Simeon said one evening. "A group of them went up to Galilee, apparently hoping to succeed where the Pharisees had failed. Their plan was to ask Jesus for a sign and catch Him that way." Simeon smiled as he looked at those gathered around him. "I'm told those Sadducees came back spluttering about how Jesus ridiculed them by saying, 'You know how to forecast the weather, but you can't discern the signs of the times!' That deputation too, ended up walking away without taking Him. Jesus told them, 'This generation shall not be given any sign except the sign of the Prophet Jonah.' "

Eli's heart skipped a beat. There it was again, the sign of the Prophet Jonah. *What could the Master mean?* Eli wondered. He waited, hoping Simeon would explain, but he didn't.

"It's no wonder Jesus has called our rulers 'blind leaders of the blind,' " Simeon said.

"A bold statement," murmured Isaiah.

Simeon nodded. "And He also warned the disciples, 'Beware of the leaven of the Pharisees and Sadducees.' "

Isaiah smiled. "You don't seem to be offended."

"Oh, no," Simeon replied. "People may still call me a Sadducee, but I am not a Sadducee at heart anymore, only in name."

Neither am I a Pharisee at heart! Eli thought.

THE FEAST OF TABERNACLES was nearing when Simeon told what happened at the foot of Mount Hermon. "Jesus and His disciples were away from Capernaum for awhile this summer, and no one seemed to know where they were," he said. "Apparently Jesus wanted to spend some time alone with His men." Simeon's eyes shone. "Preparing them for what is ahead, I presume. Later, people found out that Jesus and His disciples had been near Caesarea Philippi, and once they went up onto Mount Hermon for awhile. Actually, only three of the disciples went up with Him, for while He was gone a crowd gathered around the other nine at the foot of the mountain. A man had brought his only child, possessed by an evil spirit."

Eli drew in his breath sharply, thinking of his father. Actually, Amos had not suffered a spell for over a year, but the memory of those spells was still vivid in Eli's mind.

"The nine remaining disciples tried to cast out the evil spirit, but they couldn't," Simeon was saying. "When Jesus came down He said, 'O you of little faith, how long must I be with you? Bring your child to me.' So the father brought the child, begging, 'If you can, then do something for him.' And Jesus exclaimed, 'If I can! Don't you know that all things are possible to him who believes on Me?' Then the father cried out, 'Lord, I believe; help my lack of faith.'"

The words found an answering echo in Eli's heart. *That's like me,* he thought. *I want to believe, but it's so hard.*

Before leaving for home, Eli spoke briefly with Sharon.

"What do you think?" she asked. "Will Jesus come up to Jerusalem for the Feast of Tabernacles? Some think not because of the danger."

Eli was disappointed. "Really? I was hoping He might come."

"So was I," Sharon admitted. "I would like to see Him. But oh, sometimes I am frightened for Jesus when I hear Father talking. More than once, now, he has heard that Jesus speaks as though He expects to die soon."

Eli shuddered. "I wonder why. I can't understand it."

"Neither do I," Sharon admitted. "Surely God will take care of His own Son."

Eli marveled to himself, *She really believes Jesus is the Son of God.* He envied her faith.

THE FEAST BEGAN. Obediently, Eli built a booth for his father and slept outdoors with him at night. This made it harder for him to get away to the House Ben Asa. But one evening during the festive week he managed to go. Neither Asa nor Simeon had gone up to Jerusalem, mainly because no one expected Jesus would risk appearing there.

Simeon told of a time when the disciples of Jesus asked Him who would be the greatest in the kingdom of heaven. "The Master had a way of humbling them quickly," Simeon commented with a smile. "He set a child in their midst and said, 'Unless you become as little children, you can't even enter the kingdom of heaven. Whoever shall humble himself like a child shall be the greatest in the kingdom.' "

Later, Eli told Sharon, "I had to think of Isaac Bar Isaiah when your father told us what Jesus said about becoming like little children. Isaac is so open and trusting."

Sharon nodded. "Little children have faith. That is what we need too."

"I wish we could spend more time together," Eli said wistfully.

She looked up at him, her face troubled. "But we are not betrothed."

Eli's voice was rough with emotion. "We would be, if..."

She held up her hand. "Yes, I know. But we don't want to go against our parents' wishes, do we?"

For a moment he resented her unquestioning sub-mission. *Why can't she consider my feelings for a change, or her own, for that matter?* he thought.

"I guess not," he said reluctantly.

Chapter 21

Uncle Shem had not visited the House Ben Amos for weeks, but on the last day of the feast he came in excitedly. "The blasphemer is in Jerusalem! He is speaking every day in the temple!"

Eli shot to his feet. "You mean Jesus? Is He . . ." Then seeing the look on his father's face, he stopped short. In growing amazement he listened as Shem told how temple guards had tried to seize Jesus, but He had escaped them. Eli had no desire to listen to the tirade that was sure to come from Father, so he slipped through the courtyard.

"I have to go and tell Asa," he murmured to Mother.

He ran as fast as he dared through the darkened streets and pounded on the door of the potter's house. Asa, looking sleepy, appeared with a lighted lamp. His eyes widened as he took in Eli's agitation.

"He came! He's in Jerusalem right now!" Eli cried, nearly incoherent in his excitement.

"Jesus is up for the feast? Oh, if only I could go, but Hannah is not well, and I must stay," mourned Asa. "But Father must know. He will surely go to meet the

Master. I will tell him tomorrow. Would you go with him, Eli?"

"Would I?" he almost shouted. "You know I would, but I can't. Not without deceiving my father."

"Well, at least if Father goes we will hear all about it," Asa said. They talked awhile longer, sharing ideas about what Jesus might be planning to do.

"He seems invincible," gloated Eli. "Shem says the temple guards tried more than once to take Him."

Reluctantly, Eli returned home, but his excitement kept him awake for hours. At last, at last, the King had come to Zion! Surely this time Jesus would claim His kingdom!

Eli was plowing the next day when he was startled to hear Asa's voice behind him. "Can't you stop for a moment?" he called in mock irritation, walking awkwardly over the furrows.

Eli grinned. "I sure can. This is like old times. Coming back to work for your father, are you?"

Asa shook his head. "I'm a potter now, and my wife needs me at home. I can't stay long, but I just got back from telling my father that Jesus is in Jerusalem." A cloud passed over his face. "Too bad. But Father can't go right away. He hurt his foot yesterday."

"Oh," said Eli, disappointed. "Is it bad?"

"Could be worse. But it will be some days before he can leave."

"By that time Jesus may have gone," Eli said regretfully.

He was right. By the time Simeon reached Jerusalem, Jesus was gone. Simeon returned with glowing stories, however, and the two families gathered at the potter's house to hear about it.

"I was told Jesus said a most wonderful thing on the last day of the Feast," Simeon began eagerly. "He stood in the temple and called out, 'If any man thirst, let him come to Me and drink! He who believes in Me, as the Scripture has said, out of his innermost being shall flow rivers of living water!'"

"That was on the last day of the feast?" Isaiah asked in awe. "That is when they have the ceremony of the drawing of water!"

Simeon's eyes shone. "I know. That's what makes it so wonderful. Jesus is telling us to look to Him, not to those outdated ceremonies, which are nothing but broken cisterns. Jesus Himself is the fountain of living waters spoken of by Isaiah the prophet!"

After a pause, Simeon went on, "He said many more wonderful things in the temple. Once He declared, 'If you abide in My Word, you are truly My disciples; and you shall know the truth, and the truth shall make you free.'"

Free! Free! The words echoed and reechoed in Eli's mind, as though bouncing off the obstacles and barriers in his life. Oh, to be free!

"Then there was the day Jesus healed the blind man," Simeon continued. "Oh, to have been there! He paused beside this blind beggar near the temple, and someone heard Him say, 'While I am in the world, I am the light of the world.' Then He went on to prove that He can give light to someone in darkness. He healed a beggar in a strange way: He spat on the ground and mixed up some mud with His finger, then smeared it on the blind man's eyelids. 'Go, and wash in the pool of Siloam,' He ordered. And when the beggar went to Siloam and washed the mud from his eyes, he was able to see."

Eli pictured the pool of Siloam. Once it had reminded him of the Dead Sea, and of broken cisterns. But now a song from the Prophet Isaiah came to him. " 'Therefore with joy shall ye draw water out of the wells of salvation. . . . Cry and shout, thou inhabitant of Zion: for great is the Holy One of Israel in the midst of thee!" he quoted.

"Just think!" exclaimed Simeon. "That we are of the generation who sees the day when the Holy One of Israel walks in Zion!"

But there was a darker side to the story. Eli heard it from his mother after a visit by Uncle Shem. "The Sanhedrin was in an uproar, it seems, while Jesus was preaching in the temple," she told Eli when he came home from work.

Eli rubbed his cold hands together over the fire where supper was cooking. "I can imagine!" he said. "They must have been very upset at the way Jesus eluded those sent to take Him."

Mother stirred the lentil soup briskly. "That was part of the problem. But Shem says they even have trouble agreeing on what should be done with Jesus." She paused, lifting her eyes to her son's. "It's Nicodemus, Eli. He keeps dragging his feet when the council tries to condemn Jesus. Early in the Feast he challenged the Sanhedrin, 'Does our law judge a man unless it first hears from him and knows what he is doing?"

"He has a lot of courage," Eli said admiringly.

"Yes, and influence too. The council simmered

down, for that day at least. Some of them came up with a plan to trap Jesus and prove once and for all to Nicodemus that He must be taken." Mother smiled. "Only it didn't turn out that way. They brought a sinful woman to Jesus and reminded Him that the Law of Moses says such a person ought to be stoned. Then they asked Jesus what He would say."

Eli sucked in his breath. "I can't imagine Jesus stoning anyone, especially not a woman!"

"Jesus didn't reply right away. He just bent down and wrote on the ground for awhile. Then He stood up, looked at her accusers, and said, 'He who is without sin among you, let him cast the first stone.' Then He bent down and wrote on the ground again. One by one, those self-righteous men slipped away!"

Eli couldn't help chuckling as he imagined the scene. "So it was they, and not Jesus, who were caught in a trap."

Mother nodded. "Nicodemus may have felt that he had made a point. Then later there was another controversy about a blind beggar whom Jesus healed on the Sabbath. Most of the Sanhedrin argued that Jesus could not be from God. But some, including Nicodemus, countered that if Jesus were a sinner, He could not give sight to the blind. Shem claimed there's practically a split in the Sanhedrin, though they did manage to expel the formerly blind man from the synagogue."

"They excommunicated him? I cannot understand that!" exclaimed Eli.

"I think it goes to show how confused the Sanhedrin is," Mother responded.

"WHERE HAS JESUS gone?" Eli asked Asa one evening. "When your father couldn't find Him in Jerusalem, I thought surely He would not have gone far away. But that's been weeks ago, and Jesus hasn't been back!"

"Oh, we heard He's in Galilee again," Asa replied.

"I wonder why?" Eli said, disappointed. "I thought surely this time Jesus would stay in Jerusalem, and . . . and do some of the great things your father believes He will do."

Asa knit his brows. "You know, I get the feeling Father's ideas are changing about what he expects Jesus to do. Recently he told me something Jesus said during the Feast of Tabernacles at Jerusalem. The Master called Himself the 'Good Shepherd,' and declared He would lay down His life for His sheep."

"Lay down His life?" Eli repeated wonderingly. "What does your father think He means?"

"Well, of course, he's not sure, but . . . Jesus seems to be talking about His death, doesn't He?"

Eli stared down at his hands. "I wish He wouldn't. It scares me. What can He accomplish by dying?"

"You've heard my father talking about these things too," Asa said softly. "The sinless sacrifice for the sinners, remember?"

Eli got to his feet. "I hope your father is wrong!" he said roughly.

Chapter 22

Only a few weeks later, as winter drew on toward the Festival of Lights, Eli's hopes soared again. Word came that Jesus was in Perea, the land east of Jordan.

"He's heading toward Jerusalem," Asa assured Eli. "He seems in no hurry to get there, however, but wanders from one village to the next, teaching and healing."

"It sounds as though the Pharisees are still on the Master's trail," Simeon put in. "They are trying many tricks to trap Him. One day a Pharisee invited Jesus to dinner. Jesus went in and reclined at the table. Immediately they criticized Him for starting to eat before He had washed His hands!"

"What a way to treat a guest," murmured Sharon from the shadows beyond the lamplight.

Simeon smiled. "Jesus didn't mince words in His response! 'Oh, you Pharisees, you are so worried about the outside of the cup and platter, but your insides are full of robbery and wickedness!' "

"They must have felt insulted," Hannah commented.

"No doubt. They were quite offended the day Jesus healed a woman in a synagogue too, because it was the Sabbath, you know. That woman had been bent double for 18 years. But the ruler of the synagogue overlooked the miracle and told the congregation if they want to be healed, they should come during the six days when it is lawful to work, and not on the Sabbath.

"But Jesus rebuked him by saying, 'Hypocrites! If you're supposed to untie your ox or donkey and lead him to water on a Sabbath, should not this woman all the more be released from her bonds on the Sabbath?'"

The room was silent as everyone marveled at the power of the Master's words.

On the way home, Sharon asked Eli, "Will you tell your father about the woman who was healed?"

Eli shook his head. "It would do no good. Remember, the healing took place on the Sabbath."

Later, as he lay on his goatskin trying to sleep, he thought about Sharon's question. How different everything would be if Father could be healed! Surely then Father would no longer consider Simeon an enemy. And he and Sharon could be betrothed.

But no, Father would never consent to being healed by Jesus. The only thing that could change the situation would be if Jesus were to assume His kingship and everyone would bow to Him. Ah, what a great day that would be! In his dreams that night, Eli saw Jesus enthroned in the temple, while all His former enemies, including Father, groveled at His feet.

In the third watch of the night, Eli woke suddenly to a sound that struck fear to his heart. Father was having an attack! He pulled on his tunic and hurried down to help Mother restrain the pathetic, flailing limbs. When Father finally quieted down, Mother's face was pale and shining with sweat.

"That's the worst one he has had yet."

I'll stay home today, Eli decided.

All that day Father lay quietly without talking. The next morning he attempted a few words, but they were confused. The long days stretched into a week, and Eli continued to stay at home.

When the Festival of Lights began, Father was still very sick. On the fifth day of the Feast, Asa entered the courtyard.

"Jesus is in Jerusalem!" he whispered hoarsely to Eli. "At least we're quite sure He is. The man who told my father saw Jesus quite near the city. The strangest thing happened! A group of Pharisees had come out of the city and warned Jesus that He should stay away because Herod is seeking to kill Him."

Eli stared at his friend. "The *Pharisees* warned Him? *Herod* seeks to kill Him? But ..."

"I know. I don't understand either. Anyway, Jesus told the Pharisees: 'Go and tell that fox, behold, I cast out demons and perform cures today and tomorrow, and on the third day I am perfected.'"

Slowly the significance of Jesus' words sank into Eli's mind. "Perfected the third day? Was He telling us when He will be crowned king?"

It was Asa's turn to stare. "I never thought of that. Father said nothing of the sort either."

"But what else could Jesus have meant?" Eli asked, his excitement mounting. "When did you say that He spoke of the third day? When is this third day?"

Asa thought for a moment. "I'm not sure. Maybe it's tomorrow. Or maybe on the last day of the Feast."

"The last day of the Feast!" exclaimed Eli. "Wouldn't that be an impressive time and place to be crowned, in the temple when all those lights are lit? What a Feast of Dedication that would be!"

But Asa refused to become excited. "I don't think my father would agree that Jesus is about to be crowned king," he said, shaking his head slowly.

"I wish I could persuade him, so that he'd ride up to Jerusalem and check things out," Eli muttered.

"Why don't you go, Eli?" Mother said behind him. Her voice showed that she had caught his excitement.

He turned. "I? But I have to stay here with Father, and ..."

"Father's better," she broke in quietly. "And Asa might let you borrow his mule."

Eli wheeled about to face his friend again. "Would you?"

Asa looked troubled. "Of course, but I think you would be chasing the wind."

Eli disagreed. "I intend to find out. Tomorrow morning at the crack of dawn I'm coming to get your mule!"

Asa went away, still shaking his head. But Eli's elation could not be dampened. Dawn had not even broken when he took his scrip and hastened to claim the mule. Asa was nowhere in sight. "Probably still asleep," Eli murmured to himself. "Well, let him sleep. I'm off to the most wonderful thing I've ever seen!"

The day was chilly, and Eli pushed the mule hard, up over the twisting roads to the crest beyond which

Jerusalem lay. At the top he paused, his heart beating with excitement as he took in the panoramic city for the first time since leaving it nearly three years ago. What a stirring scene it was, and especially so when he thought of what might take place in Zion this very day!

The mule needed no goading downhill into the city. Eli steered it directly to the temple and tethered it on the outer precincts. Already the courts were filled with festive throngs, waving palm branches and chanting the Hallel while lights blazed everywhere. Eli began threading his way among the densely packed people until he was within sight of the Great Altar. Where else would the coronation of the King of Zion take place?

Time passed, and nothing happened beyond the usual bustle of sacrifices and singing. Eli circulated through the crowd, occasionally asking guarded questions. But no one knew where Jesus was. No one had seen Him today.

And no one, it seemed, was going to see Him today. Night fell while the lights blazed on. Most of the people went home. Disappointed, but not ready to give up, Eli found lodging in a nearby stable where he slept fitfully. Tomorrow was the last day of the Feast. Perhaps tomorrow.

But tomorrow passed as the day before, with no great event. Eli's heart sank lower and lower. By mid-afternoon he realized he would have to start for home. He had promised Mother to be back by dark of the second day. Returning to the mule, he mounted and rode out through the city gate.

Suddenly Eli noticed another lone rider coming

toward him. With a shock he realized it was Simeon! The older man took one look at Eli's face and asked gently, "On the way home?"

Eli nodded. Turning his mule, Simeon fell in beside him. He never asked what happened at the temple; Eli's face revealed his disappointment. After they had ridden awhile in silence, Simeon said slowly, "I believe Jesus' reference to the 'third day' is connected somehow to the Prophet Jonah. Remember, Jesus has spoken more than once about the sign of the Prophet Jonah."

"Yes," Eli said listlessly. He wasn't sure that he wanted to hear Simeon's explanation.

"Shortly before I reached the city today," Simeon said quietly, "I met a man who told me Jesus has gone away again, heading for the Jordan and probably Perea."

Eli looked up sharply. "I wonder why He doesn't stay? I know our rulers aren't very nice to Him, but He has nothing to fear, has He? I mean, He has the power to do almost anything, hasn't He?"

"Such as forcing His kingship onto Israel, even if the people show no sign of repentance?" Simeon probed.

Eli squirmed. He was beginning to realize how unreasonable his expectations had been.

Simeon continued, "When I think of all the teachings of Jesus I've heard, I don't see a Man preparing for earthly honor. I see One who loves the world and wants to save us from our sinful state . . . by means of repentance and discipleship."

Eli stared at his mule's twitching ears. He knew he

should accept what Simeon was saying, but part of him refused to do so.

Simeon's voice grew brisk. "Tell me, how is your father? I would like to help care for him, but I'm afraid he wouldn't appreciate it," he said with a wry smile.

"He's better. I can probably come to work again tomorrow."

"It will be good for you to be occupied while we . . . while we wait," the older man said softly.

Eli was touched by his understanding. Simeon knew how hard it could be for a young man simply to wait.

Chapter 23

Winter rains continued falling throughout the month of Tabeth; then, in Shebat, the almond trees began once again to bloom bravely in the chilly air.

Eli was again invited to a Sabbath meal at the House Ben Asa. "Mother, I only wish you could go along," Eli said wistfully. "You are cooped up so much, with so little socializing."

"Never mind me," she replied. "I meet other women whenever I go to draw water at the well or to buy food at the market. Which reminds me, did I tell you Lazarus is sick?"

"Lazarus?" Eli repeated blankly.

"Yes. He's the wealthy landowner of Bethany. He lives with his sisters, Mary and Martha."

"I remember now. Someone told me Jesus goes there for the night when He's in Jerusalem," Eli recalled. "He could probably heal Lazarus."

Mother nodded. "But you say Jesus is somewhere in Perea."

"That's true," Eli agreed as he hurried away to the potter's house. Simeon and Isaiah had gathered already with their families. Simeon had more stories to tell of the Master's doings in Perea: healings, clashes with the Pharisees, and parables. "Many of His parables point toward humility and lowliness rather than glory and honor," Simeon said.

Eli lowered his eyes uncomfortably. Was Simeon saying this for his benefit?

"Jesus told the people that when we are invited to a feast, we should not try to claim the best spots at the table, because 'whoever exalts himself shall be humbled, and whoever humbles himself shall be exalted.' He told the people not to invite only their wealthy friends for meals, but the poor, the lame, and the crippled from the streets as well."

"But if these are parables, what do they mean?" Asa questioned.

"I wonder if Jesus was speaking of His kingdom," Simeon said. "We are not to seek exalted positions in His kingdom. Jesus Himself is like the man who invites, not the important people, but the poor. He told His hearers about the cost of entering His kingdom. We must be willing to renounce all we have—including our pride! We must be willing to take up our cross and follow Him."

There was a silence. Everyone seemed bewildered by these last words.

"Take up our cross?" Isaiah repeated finally.

Simeon nodded. "That's what He said. I have to admit, I don't understand it."

Eli shivered involuntarily. The mention of a cross was as a cold draft invading the room.

MOTHER RETURNED from the well next morning with news. "Lazarus died. I am so sorry for his sisters, Mary and Martha. They were so close to their brother."

"They are probably thinking that if only Jesus had been here, He could have healed Lazarus," Eli said.

Eli might have forgotten about Lazarus in the following days. But one evening Mother met him in the courtyard, eyes shining with suppressed excitement.

"Has anyone told you? Lazarus has been raised from the dead!"

Eli took a step backward. "Raised from the dead?"

"Yes! By Jesus, of course! Mary and Martha sent for Him when Lazarus became ill. But by the time He arrived, Lazarus had lain four days in the grave. When Jesus spoke to the weeping sisters, He told them He is the resurrection and the life. Then He asked that the stone be rolled away from the grave, and called for Lazarus to come out! And he did—still wrapped in his graveclothes!"

"But...but...is this true? Are you sure?" Eli asked weakly.

"Oh, yes, it is true. Everyone is talking about it. I'm surprised you didn't hear about it at work. Many are believing in Jesus because of this wonderful thing," Mother insisted.

"Have you told Father?" Eli wondered.

She shook her head. "He doesn't need extra excitement."

Uncle Shem, however, was less considerate. "All Jerusalem is an uproar!" he announced upon entering Father's bedchamber.

Father turned his head. His reactions were slower, less sharp, than they used to be. "Why?" he asked dully.

"It's Jesus again. He's supposed to have raised Lazarus from the dead."

Father appeared startled. "Lazarus? But he's dead!"

"Well, he *was* dead, according to the crazy people who are now following Jesus by the hundreds and thousands. As for me, I don't know for sure what's true, but something's fishy somewhere."

"What...what is the Sanhedrin doing about this?" Father asked haltingly. "We cannot have the people rallying around a so-called Messiah. Think of what Rome will do!"

Shem nodded. "A council of the chief priests and Pharisees was assembled to address this grave matter. The feeling is that we have to stop Him. Rome will deprive us of our temple and our nation if we allow such goings-on. Caiaphas the high priest offered the solution: 'It is expedient that one man should die for the people, so that the whole nation need not perish.'"

"Yes, that is the solution," Father agreed. "But when are they going to do it? They have been trying to kill this man for a long time."

"Strong measures have been taken," Shem assured him. "A decree has been issued that anyone who knows where Jesus is must report Him so that we can arrest Him!"

The cruelty in his voice sent a chill of foreboding down Eli's spine. Could it be that Jesus was in danger after all? But no, that was not possible. Not for the One who had proclaimed, "I am the resurrection and life!"

146

STILL, JESUS did not ride to victory on this new wave of popularity. Instead, He went away to Ephraim, a town twelve miles from Jerusalem. When He left Ephraim, some people reported that He went all the way back to Galilee for a brief stay, then came down through Samaria and traveled east across the Jordan to Perea once more. Wherever He went, crowds followed; He taught them many things and healed their sick.

Then came the month of Nisan and spring. As Passover drew near Eli's feelings fluctuated. Sometimes he thought Jesus would surely carry out His plans at Passover. Jesus was very popular now because of Lazarus. Would there ever be a better time? But then Eli would remember how often he had been disappointed, and how mystified he was at the Master's way of doing things—and the hope would drain out of him again.

On the Tuesday before Passover, an unusual thing happened. Simeon himself came out to the hillside where Eli was mending terraces. The older man's eyes shone. "Have you heard what happened on Sunday?" When Eli shook his head, Simeon told the wonderful happenings of Palm Sunday.

"Jesus came riding into Jerusalem on a donkey, while crowds of people went before Him, covering the road before Him with their cloaks and palm branches! The people shouted hosannas and sang, 'Blessed is the King who comes in the name of the Lord!' "

Excitement coursed through Eli. "Why, that is just like the Prophet Zechariah said, 'Rejoice greatly, O daughter of Zion; shout, O daughter of Jerusalem:

behold, thy king cometh upon thee: he is just, and having salvation; lowly, and riding upon an ass, and upon a colt the foal of an ass.'" He paused, then asked eagerly, "But what happened when Jesus came to Jerusalem?"

A shadow crossed Simeon's face. "When Jesus came to the rise where the city comes into view, He stopped and wept. He said, 'If you knew this day the things that are for your peace! But now it has been hidden from your eyes. For days will come upon you when your enemies will encircle you, and level you to the ground; and they will not leave stone upon stone in you, because you did not heed the time of your visitation.'"

Eli frowned. "He said that of Jerusalem? And that's all?"

"Following this, He entered the temple, walked all around the porches and the courts, then went home again to Bethany," Simeon replied quietly.

Eli shook his head in frustration. "I don't understand."

"Neither do I," Simeon replied. "But I don't think Jerusalem will see Jesus crowned king, because Jerusalem is not ready for Him."

Chapter 24

Uncle Shem came to see Father again Wednesday evening. "Remember how Jesus invaded the temple three years ago and chased out the moneychangers? He did it again on Monday!" he said indignantly.

Father gestured in despair. "But the Sanhedrin! What are they doing about it? Why have they not taken Him?"

"Well, you have to realize that Jesus is constantly surrounded by an adoring crowd. Jesus could not be taken without causing a riot. But our rulers are busy laying the groundwork for His trial and conviction. Yesterday they confronted Him with a number of crafty questions designed to trip Him up and expose Him for the blasphemer He is," Shem assured Father.

"So did the crafty questions work?" Father demanded.

Father is quite sharp tonight, Eli thought.

Shem spread his hands. "Not too well. Ah . . . Jesus has a way of . . . of besting His interrogators."

Father said nothing, but the sneer on his face showed what he was thinking.

Shem's voice rose in anger. "Jesus was very bold yesterday, they said. He slandered our leaders, calling them hypocrites—blind guides—even vipers!"

Curling his withered hands into fists, Father said, "The sooner He is put away, the better. Right now, packed with a million pilgrims, Jerusalem is a bonfire waiting to be lighted. Jesus is the spark that could do it. But think of the slaughter Rome would visit upon us if there were an insurrection!"

Shem nodded solemnly. "Very true." He started to say something more, then looked at Eli sitting off in the corner and changed his mind.

"Don't worry, Amos," he said. "We have a good start. Soon you will hear that Jesus has been taken care of."

Eli shivered as he watched his uncle going away into the night. That night Eli again woke to the terrible, and all too familiar, sound of moaning and thrashing in the chamber below. Once more he dashed down the ladder to be with Mother. Father's eyes were vacant and staring; over and over he moaned, "Get Him! Get Him! He will kill us all." His arms swung wildly in the air.

By this time Mother had seen so many of these spells that she was able to remain quite calm. "It might not last long," she said to Eli. She was right. When the first light of dawn crept into the room, Father lay asleep, though his breath still came in gasps.

Mother went out to the courtyard and stirred the fire to life. Eli followed her outside. "Shall I stay at home today?"

"Please do."

Eli stood watching her rake the coals. Suddenly he

had to know. "Is it true, Mother? Is Father possessed by an evil spirit?"

Her eyes widened as she looked at him. She nodded imperceptibly. "That's what I think. But don't tell anyone."

Depression washed over Eli. How he longed to share this burden with his friends! But all he could do this morning was hurry over to the House Ben Isaiah to let Joseph know he wouldn't be at work.

What he did not realize was that Simeon noticed his absence and asked Joseph about him. Upon hearing that Amos was worse again, Simeon made up his mind to do something he had never done before. How surprised Eli was to find Simeon and his wife Lana at his door on Friday morning!

The older man's brow was drawn together with concern. "We had to come see how things are going," he whispered. "We won't come in if your father will be offended."

Eli was relieved to see his friends. "You may come in. Father is so ill that he will not even recognize you." Apprehensively he watched Mother's face as he let the visitors inside.

At first her eyes showed surprise, even fear, but she recovered quickly and gave Simeon and Lana a proper welcome. "I am afraid you will have to sit on the floor, as we have no bench," she apologized.

Simeon smiled as he lowered himself and crossed his legs. "We do it all the time at Asa's house." His smile vanished when he saw Father, pale and unconscious, lying on his pallet. Everyone was silent for awhile.

After some minutes Simeon whispered, "Is it all right if I tell you something that happened in Jerusalem on Tuesday?"

Eli looked at Mother, then nodded.

"Some Greeks who were up for the Feast came to the Master's disciples and asked to see Jesus," Simeon began. "When the disciples told Jesus, He started speaking in a very strange manner. 'The hour has come for the Son of Man to be glorified!' He also said something about a grain of wheat having to fall into the ground and die before it can bear fruit."

"What did He mean?" Eli broke in, strangely troubled by these words.

Simeon turned to look at him. "I think He was talking about Himself, and that He must die soon. He also said, 'My soul is troubled; I am tempted to say, "Father, save Me from this hour"; but no, this is the cause for which I came.'"

Eli shuddered, thinking of the Master's enemies lying in wait for Him. Could it really be true that they would triumph and Jesus would die? But why? Why?

Simeon continued, "Jesus began praying aloud, calling upon His Father to glorify His name. And I am told those present heard a voice from heaven, saying, 'I have both glorified it, and will glorify it again!'"

Eli was speechless. Mother's eyes were wide with amazement.

"Jesus went on to say, 'Now is the judgment of this world; now shall the ruler of this world be cast out! And I, if I be lifted up, will draw all men to myself.'"

The words struck a new fear into Eli's heart. "What did He mean by being 'lifted up'?"

Simeon's face was grave. "Was He giving a hint of how He will die?"

Eli stared at him as the meaning sank in. "No!" he protested. "He cannot mean that He would be . . . that He will be . . ." But Eli could not bring himself to utter the horrible word. Only the worst criminals suffered such cruel deaths. How could they hang the Son of God on a tree to die?

There was another long space of silence, broken only by Father's labored breathing. It was Lana who asked timidly, "Have you ever thought of asking Jesus to heal Amos?"

Mother's hand flew to her mouth. She shook her head. "As you know, Amos is an enemy of Jesus."

Lana bowed her head and was silent again.

At about the fourth hour, Father opened his eyes and focused on Eli. "The lamb!" he said hoarsely. "Has anyone secured a lamb for the Passover? We need a lamb!"

Eli looked wonderingly at Mother. Was Father getting better if he could remember that today was the preparation for the Passover?

Then the sick man uttered a scream, and his arms and legs thrashed convulsively. Simeon started up in alarm, but before he could reach the pallet, Father lay still again, as still as death. His breathing had stopped.

Chapter 25

The House Ben Amos was suddenly bustling with
activity. According to Jewish custom, the body would
have to be buried that day; and because tonight brought
the beginning of Passover, extra haste was necessary.
How relieved Eli was to have Simeon take charge, hir-
ing the mourners and notifying the rabbi and the near-
est neighbors. He also planned to let Uncle Shem know,
but when he returned from that errand, Simeon wore
a puzzled frown. "Shem isn't at home. His wife said
he went up to Jerusalem yesterday."

A grim foreboding jolted Eli. What was Uncle Shem
up to? He had seemed very confident the other day,
that Jesus would be taken soon. Was Shem involved
in some awful scheme?

Soon the small funeral procession wound down the
village street to the burial ground. The rabbi spoke
briefly and led in the prayer for the dead; then Eli and
Mother walked home again with their faithful friends.

"Look how dark the sky is!" Eli exclaimed. "Isn't
this strange for the sixth hour?" Even as he spoke, the
darkness seemed to swoop out of the sky and envelop
the village.

They had reached the house. "We will stay with you," Simeon spoke through the darkness. Eli was glad.

"Thank God the girls are at Uncle Adam's house," Lana murmured.

For the first time in many hours, Eli thought of Sharon. He wondered what she was doing in this oppressive darkness. She wouldn't even know yet that Father was dead.

Dark minutes dragged on into dark hours. Thunder rumbled. At the ninth hour the rumblings grew more ominous. Eli felt a tremor beneath his feet, and the whole house shuddered. "Earthquake!" he cried.

"What can be the meaning of this?" Mother burst out.

And then, like a new morning dawning, the darkness lifted and light came streaming through the windows.

Simeon went outside for an inspection tour. "The earthquake hasn't done much damage here," he reported upon his return. "Will you be all right if we leave now? We're worried about the girls."

"Yes, go to them," Mother urged.

Eli watched them leave with an unspoken longing: he too wished to see the girls, or at least one of the girls, and tell her all that had happened.

After sundown, when the Sabbath had begun, Simeon returned to the House Ben Amos with his entire family, including Asa and Hannah. The moment he saw their faces Eli knew something terrible had happened, something far worse than Father's death.

"What is it?" he cried. Beyond Simeon he could see Sharon's face, ashen with horror.

Simeon came in and sat down heavily. "He is dead. Jesus is dead." He buried his face in his hands. The women began weeping softly.

The room was silent. Finally Eli managed to ask, "When? What happened?"

He knew what the answer would be before it came. The word fell from Simeon's lips like a cry of pain: "Crucified!"

Eli wanted to rise up and shout, "No, no, not Jesus! Not nailed to a tree like a criminal!" But he knew it would be futile.

"He died," Simeon went on, "at the ninth hour. Those three hours of darkness . . . were His hours of deepest suffering. He had been lifted up on the cross at the third hour."

"Lifted up," repeated Eli, in a daze. "I refused to believe it when you told me—only yesterday—what Jesus had said. But it is true."

"Yes, it is true," Simeon said.

"But did they try Him? Had they any grounds to condemn Him?" Asa protested.

Simeon gestured toward Sharon. "Tell us what you heard."

Only fragments about the awful day had reached Ashbaroth. Sharon told of a trial before the high priest, a journey to Herod's palace during the night, and an appearance before Pilate at dawn. "They said . . . they said . . ." A sob choked her voice. "Pilate didn't want to do it, but the crowd insisted, 'Crucify Him!' "

Asa shook his head disbelievingly. "The same crowd that was shouting 'Hosanna' to Him only a few days ago?"

157

Simeon spread his hands. "We don't know. But we do know Jesus was taken to Golgotha, and there nailed to the cross."

"I don't understand," Eli said, almost in a wail. "If He was the Son of God, why did God let them do these things?"

Strangely, Simeon's eyes were shining. "Even now, though Jesus is dead and in the tomb, I still say, wait! Great things are in store!"

"I don't see how," Eli groaned.

"Remember those three days in the bowels of the earth," Simeon reminded him.

Eli's head jerked up. "You mean you really believe that He . . . He will rise again?"

"He said He is the resurrection and the life," came the answer. Simeon rose to his feet. "We must go now. But some of us will be back tomorrow. You are a house in mourning."

ELI AWOKE that Sabbath morning with a feeling of emptiness, as though his whole life were nothing but a great hollow of darkness. *Is this what grief feels like?* He asked himself as he went down the ladder. *But for whom am I grieving? Father? Or Jesus?*

But he had never even seen Jesus! Perhaps that was the greatest sting of all. This wonderful Man had not lived long enough for Eli to meet Him.

Or was Jesus a wonderful Man? Gradually, over the past weeks, Eli had been coming closer to believing that Jesus was the Son of God. Now his faith had been deeply shaken. Surely the Son of God would never have submitted to death on a Roman cross! Perhaps Jesus had been nothing but an ordinary man gone slightly crazy. If that were true, He was no better than Father had been.

For half the day, Eli sat huddled against the wall with his head in his hands. He was only vaguely aware of Mother, huddled in another corner of the room with her own private grief. Neither ate.

At mid-afternoon Eli heard someone entering the courtyard, and remembered Simeon's promise to come again. He dragged his feet to the door, then drew back in confusion. Sharon was with her parents! Strangely, Eli found himself wanting to run away and hide. He did not want her to see him like this, unkempt and depressed.

Simeon knew more about the trial of Jesus. He told how shamefully Jesus had been treated, about the crown of thorns and the mocking, purple robe.

"You know what Isaiah says, Eli. 'He was oppressed, and He was afflicted, yet He opened not His mouth: He is brought as a lamb to the slaughter, and as a sheep before her shearers is dumb, so He openeth not His mouth.' The tormentors of Jesus may have considered Him a victim, but He was actually the Victor, because He put them to shame."

"How can you say that?" Eli asked bitterly. "Was it not He who was put to shame on the cross?"

Simeon shook his head. "Even on the cross, Jesus was not like other men. He did not cry out against His executioners; rather, He prayed for them."

"Are you suggesting that He didn't suffer as much as an ordinary man would have?" Mother wondered.

There was a catch in Simeon's voice. "No, I am not saying that. He was in agony, according to those who were there."

"But why? Why this senseless suffering of a sinless man?" Eli asked wearily.

Everyone was silent for awhile. It was Sharon who reminded her father, "You haven't told Eli about the temple veil."

Simeon looked up. "Eli, the veil before the holy of holies has been torn in two."

"Did Roman soldiers enter the temple?" asked Mother.

Simeon hesitated. "Some claim an unseen Hand rent the veil from top to bottom at the moment Jesus died."

Eli stared at the floor, his mind closed.

"And just before Jesus died," Simeon went on softly, "He cried out, 'It is finished!' Not like one bewailing his end, but as one who has accomplished a great thing. Even a Roman soldier who heard Him exclaimed, 'Truly this was the Son of God.'"

"The Son of God on a cross, indeed," mumbled Eli.

Simeon didn't answer. "We should be going now," he said.

"You didn't tell him about the burial," Sharon spoke up.

"Why don't you tell him?"

She nodded. "Two of our rulers, Nicodemus and Joseph of Arimathea, requested the body of Jesus and saw to His burial."

"Nicodemus!" exploded Eli. "So now, when Jesus is dead, he finally dares come forward to do something for Him? Why didn't he stand up for Jesus when He was being tried?"

Sharon stepped back, surprised at his outburst.

"I know it's easy to feel bitter, today of all days," said Simeon quietly as he led the women toward the door. "But God can heal our bitterness. Shalom."

Eli's hollow feeling returned in full force when they had gone.

"You could have been more courteous to them," Mother reproached softly.

"I guess this isn't a good day for me," Eli said, his head in his hands.

"I understand," she sympathized. Her words somehow drew them closer, so that now they were not grieving separately, but sharing their sorrow.

Chapter 26

Not until Sunday morning did Uncle Shem appear at his dead brother's house. "We can be glad Amos is at rest," he said, attempting to comfort them. "His illness tormented him so. He was a good man, true to the Law as few men are."

Into Eli's mind flashed some of the words Jesus had used to describe the Pharisees: *Hypocrites! Vipers! Blind leaders of the blind!*

Unaware of his nephew's thoughts, Shem went on. "Yet it is a pity that Amos did not live to witness his heart's desire—the death of this traitor, Jesus. Amos longed for this. There is rejoicing in the Sanhedrin today, for a great calamity has been averted by having this Man put to death before He led us into the jaws of the Roman lion."

Strangely, Eli felt the need to defend Jesus. "Yet they say that even the Romans called Him the Son of God!"

Shem laughed harshly. "You mean the sign on His cross? That was just Pilate's little joke."

"What sign on the cross?"

"Oh, Pilate had a sign posted above the traitor's head, reading, JESUS THE NAZARENE, KING OF THE JEWS. But it was just a joke. The chief priests tried to persuade Pilate to change the wording, but he refused. I guess he felt he'd been forced to allow Jesus' crucifixion, so was determined not to change his mind about the sign."

"So Pilate didn't want to condemn Jesus?" Eli asked, wanting to hear Shem's version.

"Oh, no. I have never seen a more undecided man. Pilate gave in to the crowd only to save his own skin. In the end he had some water brought and washed his hands, claiming he was innocent of this Man's blood. The crowd shouted right back, 'His blood be upon us and our children!' "

Eli shuddered at the terrible words.

"You should have heard Jesus later on," Shem went on. "There He hung on the cross, the Man who had made all sorts of preposterous claims about being one with God. Now at last the truth was forced from Him. He screamed, 'My God, My God, why hast Thou forsaken Me?' Oh, it proved us right. It proved us right!"

Revulsion and sadness churned inside Eli. He felt like he needed to go out and be sick in the street.

Shem rose to his feet. "I must go and let you rest. You look ill. And no wonder, with the sorrow of your dear father's death." At the door he paused. "By the way, the Sanhedrin has taken every precaution so that no one can steal the body of Jesus and claim afterwards that He is risen. They asked Pilate to set a watch at the grave."

Eli's mind reeled as he watched Shem go down the

street. What had he heard in his uncle's voice—beneath that self-congratulatory tone? Was it a note of apprehension, or even fear?

Sunday passed drearily, the hours punctuated by the wailing of the professional mourners. Neighbors and relatives came and went. By Monday, Eli was ready to get away. He slipped over to the House Ben Asa.

To his surprise, Sharon met him at the door. Her face was filled with happiness. "How good that you are here! I just arrived to tell Asa and Hannah the wonderful news!"

"Wonderful news?"

"Jesus! He is risen!"

Eli stared. "What wild stories have you heard now?" he asked harshly.

Her eyes filled with pain. "I know it's incredible. But come in, and I will tell all of you."

Eli sat on a mat near Asa. *Don't forget. This is a girl whose emotions are overruling her reason,* he cautioned himself.

Sharon was too excited to sit. "The women saw it first! They went at dawn yesterday morning, carrying spices to embalm the body properly. But when . . ."

Asa broke in, "How in the world did these women plan to get past the huge stone at the mouth of the grave?"

Sharon hesitated for a moment. "I don't know," she admitted. "But there was no need! The soldiers were gone! The stone had been rolled away! And the body was not there either."

"So it happened as the chief priests feared. Someone stole the body," Eli said flatly.

"You must let me tell it all," Sharon said despairingly. She told of men in shining raiment, and of Peter and John's rush to the grave, and of the graveclothes that lay as though they had never been unwound.

"Okay, okay," Asa interrupted. "Has anybody actually seen Jesus?"

Sharon rushed on, telling about Mary Magdalene's meeting with the Master. "Jesus told her, 'Go and tell My brothers you saw Me.'"

"'My brothers,'" Asa repeated wonderingly. "Why would Jesus have called the disciples His brothers?"

"If it *was* Jesus," Eli reminded him sarcastically. "So far we've heard of only one overwrought woman who claims to have seen Him."

"The other women saw Him too! Jesus met them—Mary, and Salome, and Joanna—and said to them, 'Rejoice!'" cried Sharon.

"But has He been seen by any *men*?" asked Eli.

"Someone said Peter saw Him."

"Someone *said*," Eli repeated mockingly. "Rumors, rumors. We must not let ourselves get carried away."

Sharon regarded him with mournful eyes. "Why are you so bitter?"

The gentle reproof smote his heart. "I'm sorry. I guess I'm afraid to believe them. All these claims about being God's Son, then confessing to be forsaken by God on the cross. It doesn't make sense to me."

"I hadn't heard that," replied Sharon. "Well, I promised my parents I'd hurry right back." Then lowering her voice, she said, "I'll be praying for you."

Later at home, Eli felt a surge of resentment. *Why does she think I need her prayers, anyway?* Then, overcome with confusion and grief, he hurried to the housetop and wept.

ELI DIDN'T SEE SIMEON and his family for a few days. In spite of all the people coming and going, Eli found the days long and lonely. He was not expected back at work until the days of deepest mourning had been completed.

On Friday, Simeon was back. Eli was surprised at the joy he felt on seeing this man.

"Jesus has appeared to the disciples," Simeon said quietly.

It was Mother who responded with a quick, half-joyful "When?"

"On Sunday, the first day of the week, at the beginning of our Feast of Firstfruits. The disciples were gathered in a locked room for fear of the Jews, when suddenly Jesus stood in their midst."

"And the door was still locked, I suppose," Eli put in doubtfully.

Simeon leveled his gaze at the young man. "If the Son of God rose from the grave, I wonder if it might be different from the raising of Lazarus. Lazarus was given back his former, earthly body. They had to release him from his graveclothes by unwinding them. But the Son of God—I wonder if His body would be one that transcends all barriers, including locked doors. You will recall that His graveclothes lay as though they had never been unwound."

"I see what you mean," Mother whispered. Eli said nothing.

Simeon went on to tell of the Master's appearance

to the disciples on their way to Emmaus, and how He disappeared when they recognized Him. "Jesus interpreted many Scriptures that foretold His Crucifixion, Eli. Would you like to hear some of them?"

"I suppose so," came the dispirited reply.

Simeon explained how the psalmist had foretold of One coming to take the place of the old sacrifices (Psalm 40:6, 7). He spoke of the words of Isaiah, who had foretold that Jesus would be "numbered among the transgressors."

Then Simeon unfolded the details of the Crucifixion that the psalmist had written centuries before, about the parting of His garments, and the offer of vinegar to drink; of Jesus crying out, "My God, my God, why hast thou forsaken me," and of His resignation when He said, "Into thy hands I commit My spirit."

Simeon's eyes shone. "Eli, you know the requirements for the paschal lamb, that none of its bones may be broken. I believe Jesus was the Passover Lamb for the whole world—the soldiers did not break His bones the way they usually do for common criminals. David foretold that too, Eli, when he said, 'He keepeth all his bones: not one of them is broken.'

"You can imagine, Eli, that the priests and scribes mocked Jesus when He hung on the cross. They were only fulfilling the psalmist's prophecy, where he said, 'All they that see me laugh me to scorn: they shoot out the lip, they shake their head, saying, He trusted on the LORD that he would deliver him: let him deliver him, seeing he delighted in him'" (Psalm 22:7, 8).

Simeon looked at Mother. "The most wonderful thing of all is that David foretold the Resurrection too, when he said, 'For thou wilt not leave my soul in hell; neither wilt thou suffer thine Holy One to see corruption.' You see, death could not hold Jesus."

"No," murmured Mother. "No, of course it could not."

Simeon left hurriedly, for the Sabbath was nearing. Eli turned to Mother. "You believe He is risen?"

"Why, yes, Eli. There is nothing I would rather believe. How could He be a Saviour if He stayed in the grave?"

Chapter 27

After the Sabbath synagogue service, Isaac came to visit Eli. At first the young lad was very subdued, as though he hardly knew how to act with someone who had just lost his father. But before long he was chattering on as usual. "Did you know that Jesus died on the same day as your father?"

"Yes," answered Eli shortly, hoping Isaac would drop this controversial subject.

"But Jesus didn't stay dead," Isaac went on, heedless of his friend's turmoil. "He's back, and now He's special because He can go places without walking there. I mean, He's like God now."

"Tell me, Isaac," Eli put in gruffly. "Does your father believe this?"

"Why, yes, and Mother too! Doesn't everybody?"

"Well, does Joseph?" Eli asked pointedly.

"I don't know. He never said much about it," Isaac admitted.

Perversely, Eli found himself looking forward to being with Joseph in the fields tomorrow. He, at least, would not be talking about people rising from the dead and becoming like God.

Later, though, Eli found himself looking with distaste upon these strange new feelings of his. *I used to despise Joseph for opposing Jesus. What is happening to me? Am I becoming like Father?*

Eli was also troubled by his shyness with Sharon. Now it was he who tried to avoid her—now, when the obstacles formerly barring their way had all been removed! Why was this so? Deep down, Eli knew why. He was shying away from her faith.

Sharon came with her father later in the week. They told the story of Thomas, how he had refused to believe until he had seen Jesus.

"Seeing is believing," Eli quipped, in an effort to make light of it.

"But Jesus said, 'Blessed are they who don't see, yet believe,'" Simeon responded.

Eli dropped his head into his hands. "I doubt if that's possible for me."

Sharon was about to say something, but Simeon raised a warning hand. "I'm sorry, Eli. We don't want to pressure you. If you'd rather we don't keep you informed about Jesus, we'll try to keep silent."

Eli thought about that for a moment. "Don't misunderstand me. I want to hear it all. I . . . I just don't find it in me to believe everything."

"The more of these wonderful things you hear, the more you will be able to believe," Simeon assured him. "I know, some of the things are almost too wonderful to believe. I often think of those words Jesus spoke to Nicodemus, that first time He was in Jerusalem. He said we must be born again."

Sharon nodded. "He said we must be born of water

172

and the spirit. But what did He mean?"

Simeon clasped his hands and began slowly, "When Jesus appeared to His disciples on the day of His Resurrection, He did a mysterious thing. He breathed on them and said, 'Receive the Holy Spirit.' When I heard about that, I had to think of the creation of man, when God breathed life into Adam. If the creation was the first birth of mankind, could this be the second birth, when we receive the very Spirit of God from the resurrected Christ?"

Sharon's eyes were shining. "How wonderful, Father!"

"And," Simeon went on, "there's another Psalm, where God said, 'Thou art my Son: this day have I begotten Thee.'

"Oh, Eli, it's very significant that Jesus rose from the dead on our Feast of Firstfruits, because He is the firstborn Son of God in resurrection!"

Sharon was puzzled. "But if you speak of the first-born Son of God—will there be others? Is not the Christ the only-begotten of God?"

"Yes and no," Simeon answered with a smile. "Don't you see? Jesus called the disciples His brothers. I believe those who believe in Him are called sons of God too, born again of the divine resurrection life!"

"So how do we receive this divine life? Must we all wait for Jesus to come and breathe on us?" asked Eli doubtfully.

A shadow crossed Simeon's face. "I'm not clear on that yet. But I believe these things will be made clear in time. Nothing is impossible for a risen Saviour!" He got up to leave.

"Did you hear the Master's disciples have gone back to Galilee?" Sharon said as she stood to her feet. "Jesus promised to meet them there."

Eli felt a strange sense of loss. "So He is not in Jerusalem anymore." Then he realized what he had said. "If He's alive, that is," he added hastily.

WITH THE TIME of mourning past, Eli threw himself into the toil of the barley and wheat harvest. Sometimes when he was in the fields it was even possible to forget about Jesus.

But Simeon would not let him forget altogether. Each Sabbath he arranged a gathering of the four families—Isaiah's, Asa's, Eli's, and his own. Weeks passed with no news of Jesus, but they often spoke of Him.

Once Simeon mused, "Our wheat harvest reminds me of the time Jesus compared Himself to a grain of wheat that falls into the ground and dies in order to bear much fruit. Because He rose again, He has become the 'firstfruits.' Those who believe in Him are the 'much fruit.'"

Farmer that he was, the words touched Eli's heart. Yet somehow they seemed beyond his reach.

"I have been told of some wonderful things Jesus spoke to His disciples the night before He died," Isaiah said. "He told them that He is the true vine, and His Father is the husbandman—and the believers are the branches. Jesus said, 'He who abides in Me and I in him, he bears much fruit.'"

"Abide in Me . . . and I in him . . ." repeated Asa. "What does that mean?"

"Would it not mean the Spirit of the resurrected

Christ living within us?" Simeon responded.

Eli felt detached and confused. The parable of the vine and the husbandman appealed to him, because he had been working in vineyards for years. But he could not identify with this talk of Jesus living inside people.

Another time, the discussion centered on the torn temple veil. "I believe this was God's way of showing that the old way of approaching Him—through animal sacrifices—is no longer valid. Jesus is the way now! He was the perfect Sacrifice, the fulfillment of all the old sacrifices. Sin offering, burnt offering, peace offering—He fulfilled them all on the cross," Simeon declared.

"The more I understand, the more I see why it was the Father's will that Jesus should suffer and die," Isaiah observed.

"Suffering and death would not have been enough. He had to be raised again!" Simeon pointed out quickly. "Only in resurrection could He give new life to those who believe in Him."

Little by little, like water lapping at a sandbar, Eli's resistance to the Resurrection was being worn away. "But I still don't see how Jesus gives new life," he countered.

"The night before He died," Isaiah recalled, "Jesus promised His disciples that He was going away, but He would send the Comforter—the Spirit of Truth—to take His place."

Simeon nodded. "As the Spirit of Truth, God can live in the hearts of the believers."

"How wonderful!" murmured Lana, his wife.

"When will these things come to pass?" Asa asked.

Simeon smiled. "I am content to wait on God's timing. It will be soon enough."

Chapter 28

The "Seven Weeks of Harvest" slipped rapidly by. A few days before the Feast of Pentecost, Eli and his mother were sitting on the rooftop at twilight.

"I am surprised that you haven't asked for Sharon's hand in marriage," Mother said gently. "Nothing is hindering you now, is it?"

Eli turned from gazing over the village and looked at his mother. "A suitable period of mourning should pass before a betrothal is begun," he said.

"But that has been fulfilled," she pointed out.

"There was something else preventing me," Eli admitted. "As you know, I have found it very hard to believe that Jesus is risen—whereas the House Ben Simeon believes wholeheartedly."

"But you do believe it now?" Mother prompted.

"Yes," answered Eli hesitantly. "Though I often long to see Jesus for myself to be sure."

Mother nodded. "Well, I don't want to pressure you about the betrothal. I only want you to know there is no hindrance on my part."

"Thank you, Mother. I might go after work some

evening and have a talk with Simeon."

By the next day, Eli could no longer think of any reason for putting it off. Still, he found his knees quaking as he approached the grand House Ben Simeon. Who was he, to ask for the hand of a rich man's daughter? A servant met him at the door, and Eli managed to say, "I wish to speak with Simeon."

He was shown to a room at the back of the house, where Simeon sat at a table, surrounded with scrolls and parchments. His eyes lit up at the sight of the young man. Did he guess Eli's errand? Perhaps he did, for he said very little, as though giving Eli a chance to speak.

"I have come to ask for Sharon's hand in marriage," he said. "I know I am not worthy, and I have little to offer her in the way of a dowry or a home."

Simeon waved his hand. "You will be a good husband. I gladly give my permission, because I know how my daughter feels about this! We will make arrangements for you to take the vows of betrothal soon."

After a pause, he changed the subject. "Have you heard about last Thursday?"

"Last Thursday?"

"Jesus ascended to heaven! He came back to Jerusalem, I'm not sure when, and last Thursday, while His disciples watched, He was taken up into the sky from the Mount of Olives."

It took awhile for all this to sink into the young man's mind. "You mean He's gone, for good? I will never see Him?"

"Not now, Eli," Simeon answered gently. "He did

promise to come again sometime to take all the believers with Him to heaven. But for now, He has promised to send the Comforter. On the Mount before He went away, Jesus told His disciples, 'Wait here in Jerusalem, and you will be baptized with the Holy Spirit!' "

"I still don't understand what that really means," confessed Eli.

"Neither do I. But it's exciting to think about! At first when Jesus was crucified I was desolate because I thought His work had come to an end. But we shall see that His death was only the beginning! I believe the baptism of the Holy Spirit will usher in great blessings to many people. Jesus told the disciples last Thursday, 'You shall be witnesses for Me unto the ends of the earth.' "

"To the ends of the earth," Eli repeated wonderingly. "I wonder how that can be, now that Jesus has gone?"

"God will have a way," Simeon asserted confidently.

THE NEXT TIME the four families met, Simeon had joyful news. "The Holy Spirit has come in power upon the apostles! It happened last Sunday." He told about the mighty, rushing wind, the tongues of fire, and the many languages the apostles were enabled to speak.

"Different languages? What good would that do?" Asa wondered.

"Because Christ's kingdom is to go out to many nations! Think of it, Asa. Because of the Feast of Pentecost, Jerusalem was full of pilgrims. Many of them were drawn to the spot where the apostles were gathered because they heard the sound of the wind. Those pilgrims spoke many languages, but each one heard the preaching in his own tongue!"

"The miracles go on," breathed Leah, Isaac's mother.

"Some said the preaching was a like a great, flowing stream," Simeon went on. "And I thought of the Master's words at the Feast of Tabernacles last year: 'He who believes in Me, out of his innermost being shall flow rivers of living water!' The Holy Spirit is now that freely-flowing, living water."

To Eli came some words from Zechariah which he now quoted: "'In that day there shall be a fountain opened to the house of David and to the inhabitants of Jerusalem for sin and for uncleanness'" (Zechariah 13:1).

Simeon nodded. "A fountain opened. That describes it so well. And last Sunday Peter quoted from the Prophet Joel, where it says that God shall pour out His Spirit, and that whosoever shall call on the name of the Lord shall be saved" (Joel 2:28-32).

After a pause he went on, "And thousands called on the name of the Lord last Sunday and were baptized! The kingdom of Christ has surely begun, now that the Holy Spirit dwells in men's hearts!"

Later, as Eli walked with Sharon a short way, she confessed, "I find myself longing to receive the Holy Spirit too."

He looked down at her. "So do I. But how is it done?"

"Well, those thousands last Sunday were baptized. Father says he is going to seek baptism too."

180

"But will just anyone be accepted?" Eli wondered. "Surely only the righteous can enter the kingdom. Jesus once said that we have to be perfect, like God in heaven is perfect."

A frown creased her brow. "Yes, He said that. But I wonder—were all those thousands perfect?"

Eli shook his head. "I don't know about them. For myself, I think I am unworthy to be part of this kingdom. Just think how slow I was to believe that Jesus is risen! It's different for you. You are a good candidate for baptism."

"But I am not perfect," she objected.

"Still, you always believed that Jesus is what He said He is," Eli persisted.

"You do too, now. Isn't that what counts?"

"I don't know."

That night as Eli lay in his room trying to sleep, his sins and weaknesses seemed to stare him in the face. He thought of his resentment toward Father, and realized how wrong that had been. Yes, he had tried to be a dutiful son, but he had lacked the true love Jesus spoke about.

Then, too, Eli thought how wrong his perception of the kingdom had been. To think that he had expected Jesus to claim earthly honor and be crowned in Jerusalem! Yet Simeon had tried all along to teach him that the kingdom of Jesus was in the hearts of men. By the time he fell asleep, Eli had convinced himself that he was a very poor candidate for baptism.

Chapter 29

The following week Simeon traveled to Jerusalem and heard the apostles preaching in the temple. The next time the four families met in Ashbaroth, he had much to share. "I am looking forward to receiving baptism," he said, taking in the circle of faces, "and I hope you are too."

"What if we are not good enough to be part of the kingdom?" Eli asked.

"Don't you believe Jesus died to save the world from sin?" Simeon asked gently.

"Well, yes, but . . ."

"But you have trouble believing that He can save *you* from *your* sin?" prodded Simeon with a twinkle.

Eli smiled sheepishly. "Maybe that's it."

Simeon sat back. "Do you think Peter is good enough to be an apostle of Jesus?"

"Why, of course! He was with Jesus for years," Eli responded.

"Yet at the end, when Jesus was faced with the cross, Peter denied even that he knew Him," Simeon asserted quietly.

Eli was incredulous. "Peter did? Why?"

"To save his own skin, that's why. And because he was horribly frightened. Eli, Peter was only human, like you and me. He failed miserably." And Simeon told the heart-wrenching story of Peter's denial.

"And to think that Peter is now baptizing thousands!" Sharon commented dryly.

"A marvelous testimony of God's power," Simeon pointed out. "Peter has something more than his own human nature to rely on now. He has the Holy Spirit. And we need Him too. That is how we can be perfect: when Jesus the Perfect One dwells in us through the Spirit."

"How can we receive Him, then?" Asa asked eagerly.

Simeon thought for a moment. "On the Day of Pentecost, when people asked Peter how they could be saved, he answered, 'Repent, and be baptized, each one of you in the name of Jesus Christ for the forgiveness of your sins, and you shall receive the gift of the Holy Spirit.'"

Simeon told how the Apostles had received the Great Commission to go out and disciple the nations. "There on a mountain in Galilee," he concluded, "Jesus told His disciples, 'Behold, I am with you always, even to the end of the world!'"

Simeon looked around with shining eyes. "Don't you see? While Jesus was here on earth as the Son of Man, He was restricted to one human body, and one little country where He could walk with His one pair of feet. But now . . . now He lives in thousands of people! He has thousands of hands, thousands of feet, to carry out His work! The believers are His body now—the church, the body of believers! Truly, the grain of wheat that fell into the ground to die is bringing forth much fruit."

"And can we too," Asa began hesitantly, "expect to be baptized with tongues of fire from heaven?"

Simeon shook his head. "Those tongues of fire were a special sign of power, for the carrying out of the commission. I understand now what we must do to receive the Holy Spirit. We must call on the Lord, which means to pray to God in Jesus' name; we must repent of our sins; we must believe He rose again to become the life-giving Spirit. Then we are ready for baptism, ready to be a child of God born again of the Spirit."

As each one in the room confessed his faith, they began making plans to go to Jerusalem and receive baptism at the hands of the apostles. That night for the first time, Eli prayed to God in the name of the Lord Jesus, confessing his sins and praising Him for His saving power.

AFTER THE BAPTISM, Eli and the others took part in what the Apostles called a love feast. They explained how Jesus had instituted this feast the night before He died, saying of the bread, "This is My body" and of the cup, "This is the new covenant in My blood."

Eli remembered that several years before Jesus had told a bread-crazed crowd, "I am the bread of life. He who eats My flesh and drinks My blood has eternal life . . ." Now for the first time, Eli saw how this could be: in the Resurrection the Lord's life had been made available as food for all through the Spirit!

Hymn after hymn of joyful praises rose from the believers. At the last they sang the "Psalm of Jesus" (Psalm 22). Many cheeks were wet as the first part was sung, for so many verses recalled the Crucifixion. But then the tone of the psalm changed to one of praise and joy:

> I will declare Thy name unto My brethren:
> In the midst of the congregation will I praise
>   Thee.
> My praise shall be of Thee in the great
>   congregation:
> The meek shall eat and be satisfied:
> They shall praise the LORD that seek Him:
> Your heart shall live forever.
> All the ends of the earth shall remember
> And turn unto the LORD:
> For the kingdom is the LORD's:
> And He is the governor among the nations.

Riding home to Ashbaroth, those words echoed and reechoed in Eli's heart: *The kingdom is the LORD's! The kingdom is the LORD's!*

"Truly," said Simeon, "the words of the Psalmist are being fulfilled. 'In the midst of the congregation I will praise Thee.' Jesus was in our midst today, in our hearts, and it is from His Spirit that praise flows to God."

Eli and his mother had barely reached home when Asa appeared at their door. He and Hannah had not gone to Jerusalem, and now his face glowed with good news. "We have a son!" he exclaimed. "I am telling you first, but I am on the way up the hill to tell my family too. Think of it! My parents are grandparents, and so are Hannah's." Away he sped up the street.

Mother and Eli stood at their door, watching Asa stop at his in-laws' place, then hurry on again.

"He surely is excited," Eli said with a grin.

"I don't blame him," Mother responded. "I wonder if they will name the baby Simeon?"

Chapter 30

After his baptism, Eli thought he would never again be sad or confused or frightened. How could he be, with Christ dwelling in his heart through the Holy Spirit?

Yet the very next evening a rude jolt brought him quickly down to earth. Uncle Shem came to visit, something he had not done often in the past weeks. "As you know, my wife and I have a new baby," he explained stiffly. "That is why I haven't come. Also, I have more duties to perform for the Sanhedrin." His eyes rested briefly on Eli. "Be assured, we are mustering all our resources to fight this monstrous new evil in Jerusalem! God will not tolerate this desecration of His holy city and holy laws! These followers of Jesus are not even keeping the Sabbath anymore!"

Eli heard Mother catch her breath. His own heart beat faster. "What does the Sanhedrin plan to do?"

Shem smiled maliciously. Eli shivered. "You need not think that I will give away our plans to you! I know full well that you also are following that dead man, if such a thing is possible. Were you not baptized yesterday?"

Eli was startled. "Were you there?"

Shem laughed harshly. "No, but the Sanhedrin has informers. Oh, you just wait! We *will* gain the upper hand. We have learned a few lessons and will not make the same mistakes twice."

"Do not be afraid of me," he added soothingly after a pause. "You are, after all, my dear brother's wife and son. My main reason for coming tonight is to warn you. The Sanhedrin will have no mercy. I will be powerless to save you in the future, once they take action. Unless you turn from your blasphemy, you can expect to be cast into prison—or worse!"

Mother's face was drained of color, a sickly white in the lamplight.

Shem stood to his feet. "I only wanted to do my duty. Shalom," he said, as he walked through the door.

"You haven't come to frighten us? That's exactly what you're doing," Eli said indignantly.

Eli's thoughts churned with fear and anger. "Shalom, indeed! How can he wish us peace, after what he said?" After a pause he added, "Of course, we should not be surprised at threats of persecution. Jesus said, 'Blessed are you when men shall revile you and persecute you for My name's sake.'"

Mother nodded, drawing comfort from the words. She sounded her normal motherly self as she said, "You should go up to bed and get some sleep."

Eli was troubled as he climbed the ladder to his room, not so much because of Shem's threats, but because he had seen a weakness in himself. Surely a man who had received the Holy Spirit should not be so quickly angry and fearful again! Had his baptism been in vain? How could he be perfect if he was so easily overcome by weakness?

Eli's feet were leaden as he went to work the next day. Nor did the other workers make things easier for him. They asked questions he could not answer about the believers' practice of observing the first day of the week as the Lord's Day. "Are you not afraid of the wrath of God that is promised to those who forsake His Sabbath rest?" someone taunted.

So greatly was Eli burdened that he knew he would have to talk with someone. "Will you go with me to the House Ben Simeon tonight?" he asked Mother.

She shook her head. "I am too weary. But do go, Eli. I can see you have many questions."

He hesitated for a moment, remembering Uncle Shem's threats. "Will you be all right while I am gone?"

When she assured him that she would, he hurried away.

Just being with Simeon and his family soothed Eli's heart. He was even tempted not to ask the questions about the Lord's Day that burdened him; but he knew if he didn't, they would return and torment him in the night.

"People have been asking me why we worship on the first day of the week. I'm not sure how to answer," Eli said finally.

"Remember what Jesus used to say," Simeon responded thoughtfully. "He is the fulfillment of the Sabbath. In Him we have eternal rest! So now it is fitting that His followers should worship on the first day of the week—the day of His Resurrection. The Sabbath was a day of darkness and sadness, Eli, when Jesus lay in the tomb. His kingdom is of life, not of death!"

Simeon's eyes shone. "Oh, I never cease to be amazed at how perfectly Jesus fulfills all the sacrifices and statutes God gave Moses. Just think of the Day of Atonement. Think how the priests carry the blood of the sacrifices within the veil to sprinkle it on the mercy seat. Jesus has done that once and for all! His blood speaks for us at the throne of the Father.

"Yet Jesus was also like those sacrifices, which must be carried outside the city to be burned. He suffered outside the city, at Golgotha, for us. His flesh was torn for us, so that the veil before the holy of holies could be rent and the way opened to the mercy seat in heaven!"

"And the scapegoat, bearing the sins of Israel—wouldn't Jesus fulfill that too?" asked Lana.

Eli glanced at her in surprise. Once so shy and quiet, even Sharon's mother was now ready with a testimony of her faith.

Simeon nodded. "Perfectly, perfectly. Isaiah says that the Lord has laid on Him the iniquity of us all. Yes, Jesus fulfills all the Law of God, for He Himself said, 'I am not come to destroy the Law, but to fulfill it.' And the coming of the Holy Spirit surely fulfills the prophesy of Jeremiah, where he says that God will write His Law on our hearts."

There was another question still bothering Eli. "But what if we don't follow His perfect Law the way we're supposed to? Does that mean we haven't truly been filled with the Holy Spirit?"

Simeon smiled. "Today we went down to Asa's to see our new grandson, Eli. What a helpless creature

192

a baby is! That little fellow has everything to learn. And when we are born again of the Spirit, we are like infants in the faith, Eli. We have everything to learn. And Jesus has compassion for our weakness."

Eli felt a great relief flood over him. After a thoughtful pause, Eli went on to tell about Uncle Shem's visit.

"I see," Simeon said gravely after he had finished. "Well, we should not be surprised."

"I worried about leaving Mother alone when I came here," Eli admitted.

Simeon looked at him, then at his eldest daughter. "I have a suggestion. Why don't you and Sharon get married? There is room in this big house for a newly-married couple—and the bridegroom's widowed mother besides!"

Eli glanced at Sharon, whose face had turned a soft pink. "We'll have to talk about it," he said.

"No hurry," smiled Simeon. "Speaking of weddings reminds me of the other week when I was up to Jerusalem and spoke with some of the believers. We discussed some parables of Jesus where He used weddings and wedding feasts as illustrations. He told the parable about the king who invited the poor and the lame from the streets to his wedding feast, and then was angered to find a guest without a wedding garment."

"But why would he cast that one into outer darkness?" asked Dorcas, Sharon's younger sister. "Why was the king angry?"

"Well, the king had provided a wedding garment for every guest," Simeon explained, "but this man in his self-righteous pride, had rejected what the king had provided. What an insult! No wonder the king was angry!

"You see," Simeon continued, "this parable is about the kingdom of Jesus. We are like the poor people in the streets, and we have no wedding garments of our own. But Jesus has provided the garment of salvation and holiness for us! Without it we cannot join the feast. Unless we turn to Him for forgiveness, we are lost."

Eli thought of John the Baptist. "Didn't John say something about Jesus being the Bridegroom? I remember wondering who is the bride."

"And do you know now?" probed Simeon. When Eli shook his head, he said, "Why, the church is the bride of Christ! He cherishes and cares for His bride-to-be with a love we cannot fathom. Our time on earth is a time of proving and preparing, so that one day the church may be presented blameless to her Bridegroom."

"Proving and preparing," Lana repeated thought-fully. "That is where persecution comes in."

"Yes. But the enemies of the church can never destroy her," asserted Simeon. "The Sanhedrin thought they had conquered Jesus when He was nailed to the cross. How wrong they were! Putting Him to death was like cutting down a tree only to watch new shoots springing up from the roots everywhere."

"Or like trying to dam a great, rushing river," put in Eli.

Simeon smiled. "That's right—but the broken cisterns and the stagnant pools of the Jews cannot stop the flow of the Fountain of Life. New streams are rushing out from every side, and they will keep flowing to the ends of the earth! 'Whosoever believeth in Me . . .' " he began to quote, and the others joined in spontaneously to chant those wonderful words of Jesus: "OUT OF HIS INNERMOST BEING SHALL FLOW RIVERS OF LIVING WATER!"

Glossary

Antonia – a fortress near the temple in Jerusalem.

Bethany – a village east of Jerusalem; home of Lazarus, Mary, and Martha.

Bethesda – a pool in Jerusalem, said to have healing powers.

Brazier (brā′ zhər) – a pan of burning coals with a wire grill.

Caiaphas – the high priest of Israel during the time of Jesus.

Cana – the town in Galilee where Jesus performed His first recorded miracle.

Day of Atonement – a feast day when special sacrifices and ceremonies were performed to atone for the sins of all the people.

Feast of Dedication – also called the Feast of Lights; a festival to celebrate the rededication of the temple after it had been defiled by Syrian occupancy.

Feast of Tabernacles – a weeklong festival when the Jews dwelled in booths to commemorate the Israelites' sojourn in the wilderness.

Feast of Trumpets – also called the Feast of the New Year; celebrating the seventh New Moon since Passover, and the beginning of the farming year.

Feast of Weeks – another name for the Feast of Pentecost, when the first loaves made from new grain were sacrificed.

Galilee – a region in northern Palestine; also the name of a lake in the region.

Gentile – a non-Jew.

Hallel – a song of praise from Psalms 113—118.

Holy of Holies – the innermost portion of the temple, where the Ark of the Covenant rested.

Jericho – a city in Palestine north of the Dead Sea.

Judea – the region in southern Palestine where Jerusalem was located.

Lulab and etrog – religious symbols used during the Feast of Tabernacles; a lulab is a bouquet of branches and an etrog is a citron fruit.

Mishnah – a compilation of treatises dealing with all areas of Jewish life and forming the basis of religious authority for traditional Judaism.

Mount Hermon – a mountain in northern Palestine.

Nazareth – a town in northern Palestine.

Passover – a weeklong feast, begun when a lamb was slain and eaten in commemoration of the time when God 'passed over' the children of Israel during their Egyptian captivity; also called the Feast of Unleavened Bread.

Pentecost – a feast so-called because it began the 50th day after Passover; also called the Feast of Harvest since it coincided with the end of harvest in Palestine.

Perea – the name given to the land east of Jordan in the time of Jesus.

Pharisee – a sect of the Jews that tried very hard to keep every detail of the Law.

Rabbi – Hebrew word for Master.

Sadducees – Jewish religious leaders, including the chief priests; they recognized only the first five books of the Old Testament and did not believe in the Resurrection or in angels.

Samaria – a region of Palestine lying between Galilee and Judea.

Sanhedrin – the highest Jewish political and religious court, made up of 71 men, including the high priest, wealthy Jews, Pharisees, and Sadducees.

Scrip – a leather bag or purse.

Shalom – Jewish greeting, used both for hello and good-bye.

Shofar – a ram's horn, used as a trumpet.

Synagogue – where the Jews met to study the Word of God and worship Him.

Talmud – a collection of interpretation and commentary of the Mosaic and rabbinic law contained in the Mishnah.

Zion – 1. one of the hills upon which Jerusalem was built.

2. Jerusalem itself was sometimes called Zion.

3. another name for the nation of Israel.

Christian Light Publications, Inc., is a nonprofit, conservative Mennonite publishing company providing Christ-centered, Biblical literature including books, Gospel tracts, Sunday school materials, summer Bible school materials, and a full curriculum for Christian day schools and homeschools. Though produced primarily in English, some books, tracts, and school materials are also available in Spanish.

For more information about the ministry of CLP or its publications, or for spiritual help, please contact us at:

Christian Light Publications, Inc.
P. O. Box 1212
Harrisonburg, VA 22803-1212

Telephone—540-434-0768
Fax—540-433-8896
E-mail—info@clp.org
www.clp.org